LEAH'S HERO

RED PLANET JUNGLE BOOK THREE

MIRANDA MARTIN

CONTENTS

LEAH

*M*y head throbs in time with the screeching alarms. It's hard to breathe. The air is acrid, filled with smoke, so it's hard to see. Without warning, the room tilts crazily. As if up and down are no longer constants, the floor tips to one side and I'm sliding, along with everything else in the room, towards the wall.

I'm sure there are screams, but everything slows, and silence falls over me so heavy it's a weight. Can't breathe, can barely move. The air is thick. I'm trying to move, but it fights me, trying to hold me in place.

Scrambling the best I can, I try to stop my mad slide. I can't. My feet hit the wall, and then everything tilts back to normal. Something explodes in the distance, and then there are more shouts followed by more explosions and screams.

"Help!"

I must reach her. She needs me, this is my duty. My job. She's strapped to a gurney, under my care. I have to get her to the escape pod. In an instant, I'm at her side, gripping the cold steel of the bed.

"What's happening?" the woman asks, her face a mask of terror, eyes wide, mouth contorted.

"I don't know," I say. "We have to reach the escape pod."

Another explosion and she's ripped away from me, screaming. I reach, almost have her, my finger brushes the steel rails, then she's spinning away. My own scream echoes hers.

"LEAH!"

"NO!" I scream, bolting upright.

"Leah, you're fine. It's fine," someone says.

Arms wrap around, pulling me away, pushing the nightmare back. I cling to the body, shaking, cold sweat pouring down my back and tears streaming. Comforting, shushing noises orient me in the dark room. I shudder, panting, letting the nightmare go slowly.

"S-s-sa-sorry," I stutter, wiping sweat from my forehead and tears off my cheeks.

"It's fine," Allie says. "You're okay, I'm here."

I hold on to her until my heart stops racing, hating myself every second but unable to let go. I can't, it's too dark. So dark there aren't even shadows dancing, nothing but pitch black in our windowless room. Black like the emptiness of space.

"What was it this time?" Allie asks.

"It's… nothing," I say.

The dream is fading already, as it always does. I can't remember it when I wake up. I only know it was bad. Terrifying. Awful.

"This one seemed worse," Allie says, still holding me tight while rubbing my back.

"Maybe," I say, squeezing my eyes tight. "Let's go back to sleep."

"You sure?" she asks, yawning.

"Yeah, sorry," I say.

"It's fine," she says. "We're all having a hard time."

She releases her grip and scoots back over to the blanket that passes as her bed. I lie back down on my own, pulling the thin material up to my neck and rolling onto my side. I'm not going to sleep, I know from experience, but I'm not going to be selfish. One of us should get some sleep at least.

This is my life. It's not the life I had, not the one I wanted, and sure not any life I ever dreamed of having. In a few moments, the only sound I hear is Allie's breathing as it evens out telling me she's asleep. I lie as still as possible, keeping my eyes closed, and praying maybe I'll find my way back to sleep.

I'm so tired. Every bone in my body is weary, aching for a good night's sleep. I won't get one, which I know, but I'll try. What else am I going to do besides lie here and wait for the suns to rise?

My thoughts spin in circles, but every time they get close to the nightmare or what happened when the ship crashed, they jump to something else. I know the ship crashed, but I don't remember it. My memories have a gap in them. I was working in the medical unit when the attack happened.

I remember the alarms, smoke, screaming, then I was on the escape pod with the others. Hurtling towards what's now our new home. A handful of survivors. How many were on the generation ship? Millions, I think, that seems right. It wasn't something I ever thought about too much.

As a nurse, I know we were concerned about overpopulation. The third generation was called the boomer generation because they had too many babies. More than the projection models predicted. The ruling Council had to implement productivity limits, making it so you had to have a permit to have a baby.

That was popular—not. I understood it though. The ship only had so many resources and was capable of producing only so much more. If the population boom kept going, we'd end up in an even worse situation. No one wanted to have to decide to end a living life, so better to slow the production of new life. We still had a long trip ahead of us, after all. Our generation would never see our new home, but we were responsible for making sure our grandkids did.

Now there are less than a dozen of us. There have to be more survivors, right? It only makes sense. I can't fathom the idea that we're it. Millions on the ship reduced to eleven? I know there were lots more escape pods—surely others survived? Maybe they landed

3

somewhere else on the planet. Maybe they're close, wondering if they're alone too.

Could we find them? If enough humans survived, we could band together and then we'd stand a better chance against the alien Order.

The Order.

There's a thought to wrap your mind around, Leah. We not only successfully crash-land on a planet, the planet is inhabited with intelligent life. Intelligent life that apparently coordinated the wreck of the ship you were on specifically to get more females for breeding.

The irony of the contrast isn't lost, is it? On the ship, we had to restrict breeding due to excessive population. We were crashed to become breeders for a race that apparently lost all their females. And not another human race. No, that would be too easy to swallow.

The Zmaj are far from human. Everyone I've seen is or is close enough to seven feet tall, wide as a door, and muscled in every possible place. A fact that they seem to want to show off, because they only wear loose-fitting pants. Oh, let's not forget that they're part dragon, some kind of weird amalgamation of humanoid and mythical creature complete with wings and tail, and covered head to toe in scales.

Yet they are oddly attractive. Attractive enough that two of our eleven survivors have hooked up with a couple of them. A couple of them that aren't part of the group that caused the wreck of our ship and only want us for breeding purposes. Or maybe they do, and they're being smarter about how they get what they want.

Wow, that's cynical. I'm too tired. How long has it been since I've gotten a full night's sleep? Before the crash I know, but even then, I wasn't getting a lot of sleep. My work in the medical bay forced me to keep odd hours. My shift would swing every week so that none of us were stuck with the overnight watch. It was part and parcel of the job, but it also meant that I was often sleep deprived.

Nothing like this though. This is... the worst. Even during the day I'm starting to hallucinate. Or I think I am. I see things out of the corner of my eye. My nerves are shot. I'm scared, all the time. Scared doesn't cover it. I'm terrified. Every noise, every flash of something at the edge of my vision, and I'm frozen. Face it, I'm a mess.

I know from my training what's wrong with me. Unfortunately, having a diagnosis, naming it, hasn't given me power over it. If anything, it's worse, because it makes me feel I should be able to control it. I know what's happening, but that doesn't make it so I can do anything about it when it happens. It's one hell of a Gordian knot.

I shift and roll over, trying to be as quiet as possible, which isn't very successful. Allie's breathing hitches and I freeze, hoping I didn't wake her up again. One of us should get sleep, at least. A heartbeat passes and she's breathing normal again, so I finish rolling over.

It's so hard to get comfortable. We gathered leaves and grass to put under the blankets. It's better than sleeping on the hard, cold concrete floor but not by much. It's still chilly too. It started raining a week ago and hasn't stopped. A light, constant rain that's perfect for getting you drenched. Angota, one of the Zmaj who's hooked up with one of our survivors, Riley, says it's the rainy season.

Angota and Rakstan are the two Zmaj who've taken us survivors under their wings. I feel safe with them, mostly. Neither of them have even cast a questionable glance in my direction. Angota is hooked up with Riley and Rakstan hooked up with our own celebrity, Ziva. Well, she was a celebrity, back on the ship where stuff like that could matter. How much of a celebrity can you be with only eleven people?

I sigh heavily. Another stupid thought rather than sleeping. Who cares if she's still a celebrity or not? I don't, that's for sure. I didn't care about her 'celebrity' status on the ship, why would I start now? Yet here I am, lying in the dark debating if that status still applies.

I need to sleep. Badly.

Sometimes when my thoughts drift around long enough, I catch a light snooze. It's the best I've managed since the crash. I sleep until the nightmare comes, then I lie back down and catnap until it's time to get up.

Get up and go through the motions of another day. Another pointless, endless day that blends with the day before and right into the next. They're all the same. This place sucks. It sucks, it sucks, it sucks!

I could be thankful. I like to think I'm a grateful person anyway. I never considered myself a jerk or self-centered, at least not on the ship. I mean we survived the crash. That's something to be thankful for, right? Angota has done nothing but take good care of us. Since the other one, Rakstan, joined our ragtag band, it's gotten better too.

We haven't had any sightings of the Order patrols since he convinced everyone to move. We found this abandoned building close to the coast that is a lot better than the cave we were sleeping in. We have doors we can close so the big, monstrous things out there in the jungle aren't going to wander in. At least they'd have to knock first.

I like this building. Inside here is the safest I've felt since the crash. How long can a body hold up to being on high alert without a break? Apparently, a couple of months and more, but it really is feeling like I'm at the end of my rope. I feel stretched thin, like I have nothing left to give. I don't know if I'm going to lash out, scream, or cry, but something has to give, and it has to do it soon. I can't keep going on like this.

The others are seeing it too. I know I'm pissing them off. I don't want to. They're good people, and they deserve better than I'm giving. Everyone else is moving past it, accepting life here on this planet. Why can't I?

Why can't I let it go? Why can't I get over it and move on? What is wrong with me? Why does it have to be me who is broken?

I'm broken. That's what it has to be. Something inside of me broke when the attack on the ship happened. I don't know what, and I don't know how to fix it. All I know is, I can't keep living like this, but I don't have a way out.

A yawn comes and I shift, squirming around to try and find a position comfortable enough to let me fall asleep. The leaves and grass rustle loudly so I stop, not wanting to wake Allie up. It will be morning soon. I think. I hope. This is the worst part of the night. Knowing I won't be sleeping anymore, and now I'm waiting.

I've always hated waiting. Waiting when I'm exhausted brings that hate to a new level. A level of loathing. There's nothing I could do though. If I get up and move around, I'll wake up everyone. Then they'll hate me even more than they're starting to.

They don't hate me. Or maybe they do. Or maybe they will.

There it is. The circling drain that my thoughts sink to every single time. No escape and for sure no sleep.

This is stupid. Maybe I'm stupid. I never thought of myself as stupid before, but this is dumb. If everyone else is fine, then I have to find my way to being fine too. Except the dream. The barely remembered images that do nothing but inspire terror. My stomach drops even though I'm lying on my side. Bile backs up into my empty stomach and I'm suddenly feverish. I'm going to vomit. Struggling, I swallow down the acid burning my throat and count my way through the waves of nausea.

I'm fine. I'm not sick. I'm not sick. I'm not sick.

That's right, it's fine. Quit thinking about the nightmare. Push that thought away. There we go. Put it in this nice, dark box. Lock the door behind me as I leave it.

Visualizing myself going through the motions helps. The nausea passes, leaving me cold and feeling desperate. It's all hopeless. I'm hopeless.

Rolling onto my side I stare at the outline of Allie sleeping. I watch her chest rise and fall until I'm sure she's asleep. Then I slide my hand under my pillow and pull out the leather-bound package. Careful to stay quiet, I open it, pull out a handful of dried fruit and pop it into my mouth, rewrap the package, and slide it back under my pillow.

Allie stirs and sits up, yawning as she stretches. I swallow the mouthful of food quickly before I roll onto my back. Relief that she's waking up tinged with trepidation that she's waking up because I kept her up or she heard me chewing. The room is less dark, so it must be morning.

Less dark. What a thought. It's not dim, it's not brightening. Nope! In my head, it's less dark. I'm such a pessimist. Ugh.

"Morning," Allie says, climbing to her feet, rotating her hips, and stretching her back. A series of cracks echoes off the walls of our small room. "Ouch."

"Bad?" I ask.

My stomach clenches as her eyes pass over me. Did she pause on my pillow? Does she know about my secret stash?

"I hate sleeping like this. I miss my mattress," she says.

"Me too," I agree, sitting up.

I let go the breath I didn't realize I was holding. She doesn't know or she's not calling me out.

"Did you sleep at all?" she asks, kneeling next to me.

"Some," I say, not entirely a lie.

"I'm sorry," she says.

I force a smile. What else can I offer her? Thanks? For what? That I've become such a burden on her now, not only is she lacking in sleep, she's having to feel sorry for me too? I didn't think I could feel any worse than I do, but yup, here it is. I'm worse. I'm the worst.

"Don't," I say. "Please."

The room is too dark for me to see her face but there's enough light filtering through for me to read what's happening. She frowns and I know the rest. She hates me even more, but she'll never admit it. When there's only eleven survivors of your entire race, it pushes you to be more tolerant than you would normally be.

"We should go get breakfast and look at what we have to do for the day," Allie says, rising to her feet.

She squeezes my shoulder then opens the door to our room. The light is brighter now, coming through the open door. When I force myself to my feet, I feel the weight of the entire universe, pushing me down. Part way up I consider, for an instant, lying back down and waiting for an end.

That's not me, but that instant is undeniable.

I stretch my back and arms then follow Allie out to the common room that serves as our central gathering area and dining hall. Every step is an effort of will. My feet are heavy. Or maybe it's the weight on my shoulders.

I stare at the floor and will myself to take the next step, then the next, and the next. Allie is talking, but I can't spare the attention to listen. The wall of the hallway though, something about it is distracting. Finally I stop and stare, focusing on it. Allie comes to a stop and turns around.

"What is it?" she asks.

"Is that water stains?" I ask, pointing at the wall.

Allie walks over and crouches down. She touches the wall then runs her hand up it.

"If it is..." she trails off frowning. "Then the water got really high at one point. See this line here? That looks like staining too."

"Yeah," I say, craning my neck up to where she is pointing.

It's close to the ceiling. If the water got that high, we'd be in trouble. Some part of my mind hangs onto this, and it feels like something I should be concerned about, but I don't have the energy for it.

"We should go," I sigh, giving in to the despair and futility that all of life seems to be.

"Yeah," Allie says, still staring at the wall.

She purses her lips then shakes her head and leads the way to breakfast. We emerge from our hall together, and the others are already mostly gathered. Riley and Ziva are chattering away together, talking in a mix of Common and Zmaj.

I know enough Zmaj to pick up about every fourth word. I'm far from fluent in it, unlike Riley. Ziva is picking it up incredibly fast too. I'd probably be better if... well if I felt like it mattered. Like anything mattered.

"We need to gather more food," Asia says.

Asia is thin and her black hair contrasts starkly with her pale skin, making her look almost like a ghost or something. She's fairly flat-chested, but she has an ass that goes on for days.

"I'll go," Allie volunteers. "Who's with me?"

"I think Leah should go," Mick says, fixing me with a piercing glare.

My blood freezes. I open my mouth to protest, but words won't come out. My throat clenches shut, and tears well up behind my eyes again.

"She's fine," Allie says.

"No, she's not," Mick says.

Mick's mop of brown hair falls into her eyes, the only thing that breaks her glare in the slightest. I close my mouth, swallow, trying to force moisture back into my mouth. I can't go outside. I can't.

"Let her be," Michael says.

Michael is the only male survivor of the crash. He has a baby face with wispy bits of hair that would be a beard on any other man. He moves around the table to stand beside me.

"Why?" Mick asks, placing a hand on her hip. "Why should I? We're all pulling our weight, and she eats more than the rest of us. She can help more."

"She's hurting. It's fine," Allie says, defending me.

God! I want to crawl under something and hide. I can't defend myself. I'm worthless!

"We're all hurting!" Mick slams her fist down on the table. "We all crashed. We all lost everything. Why does she get to be a special princess? I thought Ziva was the only princess here!"

"Hey!" Ziva says, interjecting herself at last.

Everyone is angry, glaring. Lots of people start talking, and I can't take it. I cover my head with my arms and the tears overwhelm me. The dam has broken. They fall free and I can't stop them.

2

URUKOL

*M*y knife slides through the meat easily, cutting it into thin strips. The pan is hot, white wisps of smoke drifting off of it. I sprinkle the meat with seasoning, turn it over and season the underside as well, then let it set.

I dip my fingers into the bowl of water and sprinkle drops onto the hot pan. Satisfying sizzles crackle and I know it's ready. I lay the strips of meat onto it then turn my attention to the salad. Using a different knife, I chop the leaves into bite-sized chunks with rapid motions. Once finished I toss the processed vegetables into a bowl.

I turn the meat over before stirring the sauce, then chop the next part of the salad. I use a maul to smash a big handful of nuts into small chunks and sprinkle them across the bowl of salad. A quick spin of the bowl shifts the leaves and nuts around, and I drizzle a light oil over everything. Once more I toss the mixture until the oil I pressed from nuts has permeated through the meal.

After removing the meat from the pan, I let it sit on a rack to rest. While everything settles, I move the used dishes over next to my cleaning station. I lay out bowls, scoop salad into each one then

12

lay strips of meat in an interweaving design on top of each one. I step back to examine the overall effect and find it pleasing.

Satisfied, I move the bowls to the dining table. One set at each chair where my brothers will take their meal. They'll return from the hunt soon. I'm sure the hunt will have been successful. They are able warriors, after all. What warrior would return empty-handed?

Except me. I would. I'm not a warrior, though, not anymore.

My missing left wing feels like it's twisting and cramping at the thought, and I grit my teeth, forcing myself to ignore it. Times like this, it feels like my wing is still there. That the accident never happened, that I'm still the male I was.

Stupid.

The pain shoots into my shoulder. I stop moving the bowls to the table and massage it. The scar tissue twists the muscle there, making it stiff. I rotate my arm and shoulder trying to work the kink out of it.

The pain finally passes, and I sigh in relief then finish setting the table. Rain drums against the roof, some of it dripping into the living space. I'll climb up and do some repairs the next time the rain eases up. It's the season of rains, so it won't stop for a long time, but right now it's pouring down. The roof is slick, and I won't go up there. My balance isn't what it used to be. For now, I move some pots under the leaks to keep the water from spreading across the floor.

Once that work is finished, I go to my cleaning station and clean the dishes that I've used to prepare the meal. I thought my brethren would be back by now. The meat will be cold by the time they get here, which is unfortunate.

I'm drying the last bowl when I hear them climbing the path outside our home. A pang of regret stabs into my guts at the sound of their laughter and the clatter of their weapons as they enter. I can't hunt anymore. I'm grateful to them for taking me in, and I do all I can to contribute to the group, but though they never say it, I know. I'm not a man. I'm broken.

"Urukol!" Thargar says, walking through the hanging leather that divides the dining area from the entrance. "What have you made for us today?"

Thargar's coloring is bright, hued with vivid yellows and blues. He's young and vibrant in personality as well. The others push in behind him.

"Out of the door, Tharg! I'm hungry," Bahr says, bumping Thargar aside and pushing past him.

"Salad?" Dalagh asks, turning his nose up. "Males need more meat, Urukol!"

"Shut up and eat it," Othim says, whacking Dalagh on the back of the head with an open palm. "We've all tried your cooking—it's not edible. Be glad he can cook!"

"I like his food, it's tasty," Thargar says, taking his seat at the table.

"You'd eat a guster's ass," Bahr says, and everyone but Thargar guffaws at the remark.

No matter the complaints, they sit and eat. It warms my heart. It may be of small value, but it is what I can offer. I judge the reception of the meal by how much talking there is while they eat. Since there is little, I take this as a good sign that they enjoyed it.

"How was the hunt?" I ask.

"Othim almost got us all killed," Thargar says.

"Your stupidity did that," Othim says.

"Successful," Bahr interjects, pushing his bowl away. "We got a young felinus, meat should be good."

"A young one?" I ask, frowning as I rub the back of my neck.

"Yeah," Bahr says. "It was alone."

"That's unusual," I say, tingles running down my arms, so I take turns rubbing each arm with the opposite hand. "They're almost never—"

A crash and a screech cut off my words as something breaks through the heavy leather that serves as a door. A flashing blur slams into Bahr knocking him into Othim. The two males crash to the floor in a tangle of limbs.

I stumble backwards as Thargar jumps towards the dining area's doorway. All the weapons are resting on the other side. Dalagh doesn't hesitate, swinging at the blur of fur, teeth, and claws that tear at the two downed males.

Dalagh's fist connects with a meaty thud, but the felinus only hisses, apparently unfazed by the blow. It bares its teeth and snaps, forcing him to back away or risk losing his hand. Othim and Bahr use the distraction to roll away from each other and out of the immediate reach of the creature.

The felinus is large, almost two arm's length wide. It has dark stripes on its dull green fur, indicating it's a female. Flashing amber eyes dart from one opponent to the next. Its long tail twitches in the air as it crouches low, preparing to strike.

"They don't attack Zmaj!" Bahr complains.

"It's a mother," I retort. "You took it's youngling."

"I tried to warn you," Othim says.

"Sure you did, you told me how good its tender meat would be," Bahr says.

"Maybe we can deal—" Dalagh is cut off as the felinus leaps for him.

It glides through the air, front legs extending out, sharp claws glinting in the firelight. The leathery wings under its legs stretch, and it gnashes the air, pawing up and down before it connects.

Dalagh dodges to one side but not before one set of claws rakes across his chest, leaving long bloody marks right through his protective scales. The felinus twists in mid-air as it passes and lands behind him in a crouch.

Thargar bursts into the room with two lochabers in hand. I'm the closest to him, and he moves to toss the weapon to me but stops himself at the last instant. He frowns and then tosses it to Othim. My chest constricts and pressure forms in my head.

Not worthy.

As the weapon flies across the room the felinus leaps. Its jaws only taste the long shaft of the lochaber and then clamp down. The shaft snaps and the two parts fall to the ground with a clatter.

"No!" Othim yells, jerking his hand back out of the way of the flying felinus.

The felinus lands lightly on its padded paws. It spins around with a growl and leaps for me. I throw my arms up to protect my face. Its claws slide across my scales, thankfully not finding purchase but still, it hurts.

Its hot breath smells of rotten meat and an acrid odor like that of drying skins. The teeth clash as it gnashes trying to get a grip on any part of me. I push it away, falling back as I do. I come up against the counter on which I wash the dishes.

The felinus slides down, and I reach behind myself grasping for anything to hold it at bay. My hand closes on the knife I chop vegetables with. Gripping it tight I swing, leaning my weight behind it. I stumble. My balance is off where normally my wing and tail would keep me centered. The missing wing and truncated tail don't.

My foot slips on something, and I hit the ground hard. Blackness and stars fill my vision. Shouts, growls, and screams echo through the ringing in my head. My scales tingle, I'm in danger, have to move.

Blindly I roll aside, unsure if I'm rolling into or out of danger. I sense as much as hear or feel the air whiffing and scratching sounds, so I keep rolling until I hit the wall.

"I've... got... it," Dalagh grunts.

When I can rise to a crouch, I see he's wrestling the felinus. His arm is wrapped around its neck, straining to hold it. The felinus goes wild, and the two of them blur in motion as Dalagh fights to remain on top of the creature.

Suddenly he's thrown off. He hits Thargar who stumbles back. The lochaber drops from Thargar's hand and rolls across the floor coming to a stop next to me.

I stare at the weapon, mouth dry, palms sweating. The weapons taunts me. Daring me to pick it up, to wield it, to make it mine once more.

I reach for it, my hand trembling. Almost there, I'm about to touch it, then it's gone. Othim swings it deftly around, the blade whistling as it slices the air. He spins it to a ready attack position then stabs forward.

The blade drives into side of the felinus. The creature screeches so loudly my ears ring and the dishes rattle. The felinus bends in half, snapping at the pain in its side, but Othim pushes ahead, driving the blade deeper in.

The felinus growls, pawing at the weapon, struggling to break free. Othim heaves, lifting up, and the creature comes off the floor. Then it stills, dead.

Cheers erupt from the other males. I sit back and lean against the wall, not partaking. My brothers slap each other on the back with congratulations. As they celebrate, I stare into the now-dull eyes of the felinus.

It's broken, like me. It, at least, has the decency to serve a higher purpose. No longer wandering through this life for no discernible reason. At least it knows peace.

3

LEAH

"She doesn't mean anything by it," Ziva says, lowering herself down to sit beside me.

I hide my face behind my hands and try to answer, but the words won't get past the lump in my throat. Instead I choke, sob, then shake my head, all while trying to hide the tears that won't stop. They're like the rain outside. I swear, I'm going to be crying until there isn't an ounce of moisture left in my body.

Ziva places an arm around my shoulders and pulls. I resist, not wanting to be even weaker than I already appear, but she's insistent. Giving in is easier. I turn to her and rest my head against her shoulder. She holds me tight and makes soft shushing noises.

I can't hold back, and it all rushes out. I sob and cry until her blouse is wet, and only then do I sit up. I wipe my eyes with the backs of my hands then lean against the cool stone wall of my room. Ziva shifts a little so that her leg is touching mine, but she doesn't say anything.

We sit in a silence that becomes comfortable. It doesn't start there, but as the moments slip past, the soft tension and pressure that carries itself in me eases until at last we're here. Nothing more than being in the same space, one with another. I'm so comfortable, so emotionally and mentally exhausted, that my eyes drift shut.

My head nods forward, and then I jerk awake, heart pounding. Did I really fall asleep?

Self-beratement and anger flashes across my thoughts, but Ziva rubs her hand across my back and shoulders, remaining silent. She, of all people, isn't judging me. As that hits me I'm overfilled with gratitude which, of all things, brings on more tears.

I fight to hold them back, at least trying to get myself under control. I swallow hard, forcing the lump out, then rub my face and run my hands through my hair. When I hit a knot, I know I need to do something. Anything.

"I'm sorry," I say, shaking my head as I exhale heavily.

"You don't have anything to be sorry about," Ziva says.

"I do," I say. "I'm trying. I don't..." a sob clenches my throat, and I have to wait for it to pass before I can finish. "I don't know why I can't get over it."

"Because it hurts?" Ziva asks.

"You're fine," I say.

"No," she snorts. "No I'm not. I'm better at hiding it, sure, but I'm not fine."

"But... you have Rakstan..."

"And that is great," she says. "Really and truly, but not a day goes by I don't think about the crash. About those we lost."

My lips tremble as I shudder.

"You're serious," I say.

"Yes, I am," she says. "It was terrible. All of us are traumatized by it, each of us is dealing with it in our own way. Mick's way is to be a bitch."

My eyes go wide, and my mouth drops open at her bluntness.

"She's only—"

"Being a bitch," Ziva says. "Trust me, I was the queen of bitches. I am more than qualified to know one when I see it."

I want to protest, to defend Mick and her words, but I can't. It's true. Not nice, but true.

"Yeah," I sigh.

"You have to see, though, that's the point. She doesn't *mean* what she's saying, she's lashing out. She's hiding her own pain by inflicting pain."

"It hurts," I say, tears falling again.

"I know," Ziva says, pulling me back into a hug. "I know."

She rubs my back and holds me tight until I stop sobbing again.

"But you have to do the best you can do," she says when I stop at last.

I sit up straight and wipe the new tears away.

"I'm not pulling my weight," I say.

"No," Ziva says, and pain stabs into my chest. "You're not, but you're trying. You're getting better. I see it, and so do the others."

"I'm so sorry," I say, wrapping my arms around my chest.

"I don't want you to be sorry," she says wiping a tear off my cheek. "I want you to keep healing. Keep trying. One day at a time is fine, if you're getting better every day. If you're going along in an unending funk that's only getting worse..."

She trails off and I'm left hanging, waiting for her next words.

"Yeah?" I ask at last.

Ziva shrugs, flashes her brilliant smile.

"Well, then what do I do with you?" she asks. "It's not like we have any counselors, or anyone who knows how to help."

"Yeah," I snort. "We're on our own."

"Exactly," she says. "So you have to get better. We'll help, but I can't lose you. I need you."

She looks at the far wall and shakes her head, softly repeating to herself what she said.

"What?" I ask, confused by what she's doing.

"I need you," she smiles. "It's... I never..."

"You never what?" I ask.

"I've never admitted something like that," she says. "See? We can all be better than we were. There's still hope, if a bitch like me can get better then you're miles ahead of where I started."

"You're not a bitch," I say.

"Not anymore," she agrees. "But girl, on the ship? I was the best of the best bitches. Mick wouldn't hold a candle to me."

I laugh and so does Ziva. Some of the weight crushing me down eases. It's not gone, but it's less. I'm not as crushed as I was, at least.

"I think…" I hesitate, looking at my own decision and what I'm about to say before committing myself. "I think I can help Allie."

Ziva arches an eyebrow looking me over. "Are you sure?"

"No," I snort shaking my head. "But I'll try."

"That's all any of us can ask," she says. "Even Mick."

We laugh together, and it feels good. Cleansing. A relief from the constant storm clouds that fill my thoughts. The dark swirling mist that seems ready to invade any moment. Like shadows that dance in the corner of your vision, it's there waiting for any chance to pounce. Having it gone, even if it's temporary, greatly lifts my spirits.

"Thanks," I say.

"For what?"

I shrug and shakes my head. "For… being here? Not hating me?"

"Like I said, be glad you got the new me," Ziva smiles. She pushes herself to her feet then offers her hand to me. "Come on, there's lots to do."

"Right," I say, accepting her hand.

We leave my room, the safe space I'd retreated to after my confrontation with Mick. I wrinkle my nose at the musty odor, and there's a hint of wetness to it as well. I shouldn't be surprised, since it hasn't stopped raining in what feels like forever, so of course there's too much humidity.

The hair on my arms stands on end as we get closer to the main room. Will they really be okay? Will Mick yell at me again? I take a deep, shaky breath, then let it out slowly trying to calm my nerves.

Inside our stolen compound, it's dim even at the brightest part of the day. Since the rain started, it's worse. Throughout the building there are hidden windows that let the light in without letting you see out. It's clever, and I'm sure serves for protection. The kind of thing I never would have thought of before this planet.

This planet of violence and imminent death at every corner. Our Zmaj protectors, which is how I've come to think of them, have carefully taught us which plants to avoid, because even the plants here want to eat you.

We're still exploring our new home. There are parts of it none of us have entered yet. The dragon-men blocked off the section we're using to live in to make sure no surprises could find us, and we've been working to make it inhabitable. I'm glad we found something before this eternal rain set in. The cave we were living in would have been wet. When it had rained the water would run from the opening and throughout in tiny rivers soaking everything. It was miserable. This is less miserable at least.

The end of the hall is in sight, where it opens up onto the main room. Where everyone will be waiting. I stop, heart racing. I can't catch my breath and I'm getting dizzy.

"Hey," Ziva says, turning and taking hold of my arms.

I can't meet her eyes. Can't focus. Blood pounds in my ears.

"No—" I'm shaking uncontrollably.

"Allie," Ziva says, tightening her grip.

She puts her hand under my chin and forces my head up until I meet her eyes. She glistens through the tears filling my eyes. Her smile is dazzling with too-perfect, brilliant white teeth. She wipes tears from my cheeks then rests her hand on my face.

"I'm… sorry…" I sob.

"No," Ziva says, brow furrowing and her mouth turning down at the corners. "Enough with the sorry."

A sharp pain pierces my chest, driving into my heart. It's enough of a shock it cuts through the cacophony of voices telling me I'm going to die, that I'm not good enough, and that they all hate me anyway. I'm left breathless and wide-eyed.

"I mean it," she says. "It's okay that you're hurting. The sooner you understand that, the sooner you quit trying to hide from it, the better. You got that?"

"Ye-ah," I say, still trembling.

"Good. You can't heal if you won't admit that you need healing," she says. "Now come here."

She pulls me into a hug, squeezing me so tight I feel, for an instant, safe again. Maybe she's right? The noise in my head, the constant buzz of fear and uncertainty has receded, for the moment at least.

I dry my eyes with a sleeve, rub my face to try and ease the flush, then swallow hard and nod.

"Right," I agree.

She pulls me forward and kisses my forehead. "I know it's rough. You got this."

Squaring my shoulders, I nod, and she turns, leading us the rest of the way. My stomach churns, cold sweat runs down my back, and every step is heavy. I feel I'm walking to my own execution, but I'm walking it. I'm upright, back straight, head held high. That's the best I've got.

We emerge from the hall to the main room and everyone is there. Instantly all their eyes are on me, and my skin crawls. A voice is screaming to run, hide, get out of here! and I'm frozen. I can't take a step forward. Can't move. Can't even breathe.

Ziva keeps walking then four steps ahead of me she stops and glances back. She looks from me to everyone else in the room, placing a hand on her hip. She frowns and her eyes turn hard as she looks at every one of them.

"If one of you," she says, in sharp, clipped words. "Has something to say, then do it, *now.*"

She ends her statement with Mick. The two of them glare at each other for an eternity of time that crawls past like razor blades slicing my skin. Finally Mick smiles and shakes her head. It's a fake smile, or it looks like that to me, but it's a smile.

"No problem here," she says.

"Good," Ziva says. "No one here is any better than anyone else. We're all coping the best we can, and we need to help each other."

"I agree," Riley says, speaking up for the first time. She moves to stand next to Ziva.

She's pale and fidgety, giving away her nerves, but she doesn't let them stop her. Warmth rushes through my body watching her, and I wish, with all my heart, I could be as brave as her. Ziva is a natural, she's in her element with all eyes on her. Riley isn't, not at all, but she is doing it. A murmur of agreement goes around the room. Some nod and most return to their work.

"Yeah!" Michael exclaims loudly then he bounds across the room to stand next to me.

My cheeks flush hot. I look around for a place to hide or get away. He puts his arm around my waist and raises his other hand, waggling his finger at the group. I could die.

"We need to be nice to each other," he admonishes everyone. "It's tough. We'll get through this together."

The girls stare at him. My skin crawls, being at the center of this much attention. I've never been comfortable with it, and now with all my problems it's even worse. When I received an award for my work as a nurse, they wanted me to make a speech in front of my peers, and I threw up before I could go on stage. That same sensation is happening now.

A bang breaks the moment, then Rakstan enters from the hall that leads outside. He's dripping water on the floor, carrying an armload of wood. He stops as he enters and looks around at the standoff happening between us humans. His wings rustle, and his tail is twitching back and forth with a swishing sound as it moves across the floor.

"You're getting the floor wet!" Ziva exclaims, breaking the strange moment.

Rakstan looks from his mate to the floor. She spoke in a mix of human and Zmaj, using some of the few words in Zmaj I know.

Rakstan frowns at the growing wet spot on the floor where water is pooling off of him. Then he shakes.

Water flies off of him like a dog, landing on everything and everyone within ten feet of him. Cries of dismay and protest explode as people raise their hands to block the water and rush to move away. Rakstan's smile goes from ear to ear. Silently he carries the wood over to the stack we keep next to the stove, and then he turns to Ziva. In a single stride he closes the distance between them and sweeps her into his arms.

He kisses her with wild abandon. Uncaring of the eyes on them. His passion fills the room, crashing against me like the waves of an ocean. Unbound, beyond comprehension in its depth. She wraps her arms around his neck, and he spins her around and around as their kiss continues. My chest burns watching them.

To have a man who looks at me like that... who loves me like that... but it can never be me. Staring at my feet I squeeze my eyes shut and try to steady myself. Only when I hear him put her back on her feet do I open them and look up.

The best part of the entire scene is it took everyone's attention off of me. I'm grateful for that. Everyone is working, cleaning, scrubbing, organizing. Allie is sorting a pile of vegetables, so I walk over to her.

"Hey," I say, motioning with a hand as I try to push past the cold knot of fear that is screaming at me to run and hide.

"Hey," she responds, flashing a brief smile before returning her attention to the work she's doing.

The lump in my throat is too thick. I swallow several times before I can force words out.

"So, I can help, I can do this, I'm sorry about the, I want to contribute, to help, so maybe we can go and you know, get the, well I don't want to be a downer so can you, could we go and get the vegetables?"

It rushes out of me in a confused, babbling mess. Allie watches, eyes widening, a grin forming on her face. Her lips part, my heart pounds, waiting for the admonition to come.

"Sure," she says.

I almost collapse to the floor as relief floods me.

"Yeah?" I ask, afraid to believe she means it after my earlier meltdown.

She stops what she's doing and looks at me. "Yes, I'm sure."

She smiles and then slides the leafy vegetables she's working over into a crate. After she sets the crate aside, she places a hand on my shoulder.

"We got this," she says.

I hope she's right, but I don't share her confidence. Outside is terrifying. The two of us out there alone? I don't think there's enough training to ever consider it safe. The cold certainty in my gut tells me we don't have a clue what we're going to be facing.

4

URUKOL

*E*yes closed, I listen to the sounds of the early morning. This is my favorite time of the day. It's quiet. In these early hours, before the suns rise and the day begins for everyone else, I find the only peace I'll know for the day.

I grit my teeth and ignore the itching where my wing should be. I resist as long as I can before giving in and scratching the scars. It eases it, some, but never gets rid of it. That ache, it's an emptiness, something that should be and isn't.

I rise from my pallet and carefully pick my way along the wall and out to the kitchen area. I don't want to wake anyone up. This is my time. Me and the food that I'm going to prepare. It's a ritual. I find solace in my rituals, a balm for my soul. They've helped me to keep pushing forward after my accident.

My accident. My death is a more accurate description. The members of the Order were told that's what happened to me. That I died of my wounds. The sting of that betrayal is as fresh today as it was when it happened years ago. The truth is the Eye didn't think I was useful, being maimed and imperfect. He had no further use for me and banished me.

If Thargar and Dalagh hadn't found me, I'd be dead. I was still wounded when I was taken deep into the jungle, far from the Order's compound and left to survive or die on my own. So much for my brothers in arms.

As I've found out since, my true brothers never knew the truth about what happened to me. I think that no one beyond the Eye and his two rabid enforcers, Zirthoan and JKaran know the truth. Those two were the ones who carried me on a stretcher out into the jungle and left me to fend for myself.

The memory hurts even now. I begged them not to leave me. In that moment of weakness I debased myself to begging for my life. It haunts me still but their reaction haunts more. They not only smiled, it was a gleeful, joyous smile as they watched me grovel. They took pleasure in my pain and my despair.

Looking back, it shouldn't have surprised me. As the Eye's enforcers, their job was to dole out punishment, but it was common talk among the Order that they enjoyed their work too much. It was different than punishment—for them it was pleasure. It wasn't pride in a job, it was sadistic. It was evil.

Evil at the heart of the Order, in its very core. They were evil and the Eye knew it, which could only mean... cold chills spread across my arms and even out onto the missing end of my tail. The phantom part that I still feel, even though it's been gone for so long.

The others with me have similar stories, though for different reasons. Living with these males, I've come to understand that the Order is not the ideal I believed it was. It's not the organization I joined, the one I believed in and followed. Followed blindly.

I was there when this Eye ascended after the death of the previous Eye. No one questioned it then, but now I think we should have. We were blind. Trusting in our brethren, in the system long before laid down. In the ideals that we, the Order, stood for and against.

We were fools. Blind, stupid fools. Now we've paid the price. This is a pointless exercise now. Tajss is dead. Most life was wiped out by the Devastation. I no longer believe in the visions of the Eye or the teachings of the Order that a great reawakening will come. It was a lie. A lie we all believed, but nonetheless a lie.

How many people have to buy into a lie to make it true?

I know the answer to my own question. No matter how many people believe, the truth simply is. It doesn't matter how incredible or unreal it might seem, the truth is the truth. Everything else is as nothing.

I wash my face with cold water from the pitcher we keep in the bathroom then go to the kitchen. I look through the cabinets and jars to get a feel of what we have on hand for me to prepare. I find eggs and some smoked meats that will make a good meal. If we had some talik it would accent the meal, rounding it out for them.

The jar I keep talik in is hidden behind several others. I dig my way back to it and open the lid to find an empty jar. I must have used the last of it last week. I look at the eggs and meat, frowning. It's a meal, yes, but not a tasty meal. It isn't worthy of my brethren. I want them to feel well cared for, to know that I value and appreciate them.

Talik isn't hard to gather and there is usually some growing not far from our home here. I look at the door out of the dining area. Lochabers hang on the wall next to it, ready for use. My stomach churns, but I can do this. It will be fine.

Steeling my nerves, I walk to the wall and reach out my hand. It's not like I lost an arm. I have both of those, and that is what a Zmaj male uses to wield a lochaber. I tell myself this over and over, but beneath my own thoughts is the truth.

Wielding a lochaber takes more than two arms. It's balance and motion, a delicate dance between you and the weapon. The enemy doesn't even factor into it. The beauty of this weapon is the motions between it and the wielder. I'd trained with one since I was big enough to hold one up.

As my hand closes on the smooth shaft, memories flood my thoughts. The first time I held one, my first spar, my first kill. The first time I realized I couldn't wield one effectively any longer. When I dropped my weapon mid-motion.

The wood is cool, long, and smooth. I pull it off the wall, gripping tight as I draw it to me. The shaft is two arms lengths perfectly weighted to offset the blade. The blade is slightly curved, mounted into the wood itself then bound tightly with strips of leather. The outer edge of the blade glints in the soft light, sharp enough to cut a hair.

This weapon is well cared for, as it should be. A lochaber is a male's life. It is his mate. His protection and his status. It is the thing he will use to provide for his family and to defend his honor. A lochaber is not to be taken lightly.

I wish I could wield it as I used to. It feels like I can. The knowledge is there, the memory of wielding it with highly drilled skill, but I know that when it counts, I'll misstep. It's happened every time. I squeeze my eyes shut and move to put it back on the wall, and then I stop myself.

No.

Going outside is dangerous. I can't go out without a weapon. I force my eyes open and stare at the lochaber. It taunts me. Daring me to wield it, to hear it sing through the air as it and I dance. The call is strong, but I put it back into its place.

I return to the kitchen and pick up two large blades I use for harvesting meat. I slip each one into its sheath before sliding them into the rope of my pants. These are an appropriate weapon for a half-male like me. I can wield them without worry, and they should be enough to protect me if anything does happen outside. I can also use them to harvest the talik.

Satisfied, I walk out the door, pausing for only a moment by the lochabers. They taunt me as I pass. I stare straight ahead and ignore their taunts. It is best to accept what is. It's the best way to survive.

Outside the rain is light and refreshing, though it makes it cold. Keeping my head down, I make my way along the trail toward where I saw the talik growing. When I get there, the area has been rooted up and there is no talik.

Kneeling, I touch the tracks, recognizing the marks of a vier, which is not something I want to run into on my own, armed with kitchen knives if I can avoid it. If I don't scare it or interrupt its meal, it shouldn't bother me.

The patter of the rain on the leaves overhead is soothing. Water drips down onto my head, and I wipe it away from my eyes. Staring through the thick trees and vegetation I sigh. Moisture glistens in the soft light that manages to filter through the overhead clouds and the tree canopy overhead.

I've never liked this continent. It's barely big enough to be called one. I came here years ago now, and while I've adjusted to it, that's a far cry from enjoying it. I miss the warmth of home. It's damp and cold here too much of the time.

Shaking my head, I push aside a lifetime of regrets and make my way through the jungle. There's another spot where I know talik grows. I've come this far, I might as well get what I came out here for. My brothers will appreciate it—they always do—and it's the least I can do in return for their care.

The path I'm following is barely enough to be called that. It's more of a game trail where some of the larger creatures make their way through, breaking branches and pushing aside the brush. I pick my way carefully along. It's too easy to lose my balance. I'm always slightly off without my wing and the missing end of my tail. I'm not sure which makes it worse.

As I climb around the bole of a tree, there's a strange noise deeper in the jungle. Stopping with one hand on the rough bark of the tree, I tilt my head and listen. It comes again. A high-pitched sound, one I've never heard.

Some dim memory tugs at my attention but there's a note to this sound that calls to my dragon. Desperation and fear. It doesn't sound like an animal but no Zmaj could make such a sound. Whatever it is, I have to know.

I make my way as quickly as I can towards the sound. I'm not fast normally but I move as fast as I can. The sound keeps coming and now it's echoing off the trees. It's definitely high-pitched and most assuredly a sound of fear.

It comes again and my blood chills, tingles running across my scales. The dragon roars and I abandon caution, running through the jungle towards it. I slip and slide, barely keeping myself upright as I move. Each step is treacherous with loose mud or slick leaves that have fallen from overhead.

I ricochet off of trees as I crash towards the sound. It's louder and louder, echoing in my ears. My hearts pound as I rush, muscles tingling with a life they haven't felt in years. Almost I'm a male. Almost.

As I round a tree I break into a clearing and skid to a stop in the mud.

Two... creatures? One of them holds a large branch and is wielding it wildly, desperate to hold off a harimauz. The harimauz is a big one, not the biggest I've seen, but no less dangerous for that. To be holding it at bay with a stick?

The creatures holding it back, they're similar to a Zmaj but tiny. Half or quarter the size of a Zmaj, like children but they have no scales, no wings, and no tails. Something about their features screams female to me. Maybe it's their scent on the air or their eyes.

They are female. Similar to, but not Zmaj. Aliens.

Aliens warring against one of the most dangerous creatures in the jungle. Even full-grown Zmaj males try to avoid taking on a harimauz alone. The smaller of the two has fallen and is scrambling backwards, slipping in the mud. That one has blondish hair but is pale and screaming. I note her, but it's the other that holds my attention.

The moment I lay eyes on her, my dragon roars. My hearts pound as if trying to break free. The air becomes too thick to breathe, and my prime cock stiffens. She's the larger of the two females with vivacious curves accenting the femaleness of her form. She is fierce, shouting her defiance while wildly swinging the large limb.

The harimauz crouches, watching her motions, judging as it waits for its opening. Any moment it will pounce, and that stick will be of no use. Fear holds me frozen for an instant. The harimauz's muscles tense, preparing to leap, and there is no time for thought or consideration. This is a time of action. A time for a male.

I yank the two knives from my waist and rush ahead, shouting. My foot slips in the mud and I lurch forward, almost falling, but I'm able to keep myself upright. The harimauz turns at my shout, unprepared for another to interfere with its meal.

It growls, showing rows and rows of teeth behind the two long incisors that grow down from the top of its mouth. Its mouth opens impossibly far, and it roars, then leaps.

I raise the two knives as the creature slams into my chest. It's claws rip into flesh as we fall entangled. My breath whooshes out when I hit the ground. The harimauz's weight crushes my chest.

It claws, bites, and struggles wildly and it's all I can do to keep its teeth and claws away. I try to roll, hoping to get on top. I grab the fur next to its head, holding the mouth at bay. My hand slips, and the head drives forward. Pain blinds me as sharp teeth close on my shoulder. I roar in rage and agony.

I slam my fist against its head, over and over until it lets go. Its massive head rears back, mouth open, saliva dripping off its fang-like, overgrown incisors. It hisses and snaps forward, trying to get my neck.

I bring my arm around to protect my neck. Its mouth snaps shut and bone crunches in my arm. Our eyes meet and for an instant time is frozen. I stare into the eyes of doom. Cold, heartless, interested only in feeding its belly.

This could be my end. The suffering and the empty, pointless life I've lived since my wounding could be over. Seeing an end to the long road is inviting, for a moment.

"No!" one of the females screams jerking me away from that dark edge.

That is my purpose. I am not worthy of a mate myself but that doesn't lessen my duty to protect them. Fire burns in my guts, boiling my blood, warmth rushing through my limbs. Pain can't stop me. No matter its agony, I must win.

I try to find my knife with my free hand while holding the creature off of me with my other arm trapped in its mouth. Mud, leaves, sticks, no knife. Desperation drives me as the harimauz shakes its head, attempting to tear my arm off for its meal.

My hand touches the cold bone hilt of one of my knives. As my fingers close around it, a thrill rises. At first I fumble my grip, but I pull it closer and close my hand on it.

The harimauz claws at my chest with fore and rear paws. Long cuts form. I'm bleeding everywhere. My hearts pound. My vision is red, but gray is covering the edges. My awareness is slipping. I have to end this. Now.

Tightening my grip, I grit my teeth and swing. The knife drives into the side of the harimauz's head. Its jaw goes slack, and my arm falls free, limp and useless. It collapses, dropping on top of me.

Gasping for air, I struggle to get free. The slick ground is impossible to get purchase on. The weight of the massive harimauz pins me. My vision swims and I black out for an instant, but I can't. Not yet.

Females. Must. Care. Females.

Can't think. Fight. Get free.

I struggle, pushing the monster off at last, my leg sliding free. I rise up to my haunches, but another wave of dizziness hits me as the pain becomes excruciating. Gritting my teeth, I ignore the sharp throbbing coming from my arm. The long cuts up and down my body drip blood. None of that matters.

In an effort of will I force my vision to clear. The females stand side by side, gripping each other, staring at me wide-eyed.

"Are you Order?" the beautiful one with the luscious curves asks in Zmaj.

She knows my language?

"No," I answer, swaying.

"You're hurt," she says.

"Yes," I agree. "I think I am."

The knife slips from my hand. I can't keep my fingers closed, they're numb and tingling. The curvy female takes a step forward. My dragon rumbles, wanting her, desiring, but the blood loss is overtaking my ability to react.

"Leah, wait," the other female says, holding onto her arm and pulling her back.

"He's hurt," Leah says.

"He might be with the Order," the other says.

"It doesn't matter," Leah says. "I can't leave him like this, can you?"

The other female bites her lip then shakes her head. They approach, and as they do blackness blankets the world.

5

LEAH

I can't take my eyes off the Zmaj before us. He's different than any of the others of his species I've seen. There's something about him that calls me. Butterflies dance in my stomach, my hands shake, and cold sweat drips down my back.

The jungle cat-like monster lies dead a step behind the man. Its eyes are glassy, where moments before they were glinting and terrifying. I wrap my arms across myself before I take a step forward. Allie grabs my elbow and pulls back.

"Leah, wait," she says.

"He's hurt," I say.

"He might be with the Order," Allie says.

"It doesn't matter," I say. "I can't leave him like this, can you?"

I tear my arm free and take a step towards the Zmaj. He's weaving on his feet, blood running down from multiple wounds. His right arm hangs to one side with a crook in it that makes my stomach turn to look at. I'm sure it's broken.

"Be careful," Allie hisses, right behind me.

"I will be," I say, glancing backward.

Out of the corner of my eye I see him drop. He collapses like a sack of grain. Crying out in surprise, I close the last few steps and drop to my knees in the mud next to him. My hand trembles as I touch his neck, looking for a pulse. He's cool to the touch, too cool. Nothing. I wait, holding my breath.

He can't be dead. He saved us. He has to be okay.

There's a thump under my fingers and his chest rises then falls. Shallow but he's alive. I let out my breath in a sharp exhale and look up at Allie.

"What do we do?" I ask.

A cold drizzle continues to fall, drenching everything. The mud squishes as Allie kneels down. Together we push him over onto his back. Only then does it hit me he's been badly scarred and he's missing a wing.

"What happened to him?" Allie whispers.

"I don't know," whispering too, though I don't know why.

So we don't wake him? Which is ridiculous, obviously, because he's out. He's not only out, he's hurt, bad. Whatever it feels like the right thing to do.

"Those scars," Allie says, pointing at what she means.

It's obvious they're old and that they didn't heal well. The skin is puckered and angry across his left shoulder and down to his pec muscle. He's coated in blood that is still running from the open wounds too.

"Yeah," I say, shaking my head. "But the new wounds are what matters. We need to stop the bleeding."

"Should we?" Allie asks, meeting my eyes.

"Are you serious?" I ask, mouth agape.

"What if he's Order?" she asks.

"He said he wasn't," I say.

"And would he say he was if he was?" she asks.

My head explodes. I can't believe she's arguing this point. We can't leave him here. He's hurt.

"He saved us," I say.

"What if he did it to take us back?" she asks. "I'm sorry, I'm not trying to be... mean..." Her eyes drop away. "I'm scared. I don't

37

want to be breeding material for these guys."

She half-motions at the Zmaj.

"One way or another," I say. "I can't live with myself if we leave him here. We need to tend his wounds and get him back."

"How?" Allie asks.

Frowning I turn my attention to that very real problem. He's huge, like most Zmaj, much, much, bigger than us, even both of us put together. Moving him isn't going to be easy.

"We'll make a travois," I say.

"A tra-wha?" Allie asks.

"My dad loved vids with cowboys and Indians," I explain.

"Cowboy and what?" she asks, furrowing her brow.

"Never mind," I say, shaking my head. "Let's at least slow the bleeding and then I'll show you."

"How?" she asks.

I frown, considering. It's not sanitary by any means, but it will be effective. "Mud."

"Mud?"

"Yes," I say. "Pack the wound with mud. I'll deal with whatever comes after."

We set to work. It doesn't take long before he's covered in mud, hiding the scars from his previous wounds and the new ones as well. At least he's not going to bleed out on us. Now to build a way to take him back to the compound.

"We'll need some strong branches and vines," I say, searching the jungle around the small clearing we're in.

"I wish Mick had kept her damn mouth shut," Allie mutters.

"Huh?" I ask.

"She pushes you to go out to help and this happens," Allie says, shaking her head. "I mean all the gathering expeditions I've done with everyone else, nothing more than a few scratches. I go out once with you, and we get attacked by an animal and rescued by... whatever this guy is."

The smile on her face takes the sting out of her words.

"Sorry?" I say, shrugging my shoulders.

"You should be," she laughs. "I mean seriously, does trouble, like, follow you?"

The painful memory throbs in the back of my head, but the immediacy of the situation we're in doesn't allow the luxury of wallowing in self-pity. I push it away.

"It sure seems to," I say.

"All right, show me what to do," Allie says.

She follows my instructions as if I know what I'm talking about. I've seen these things in vids which doesn't mean they're really a thing at all. It sure doesn't mean I know what I'm doing to build one.

It takes some time, but we manage to get something together that looks like it will work. We've bound the Zmaj to a framework of two long sticks with lengths of vine.

"Well if he does have bad intentions, we've at least tied him up," Allie says.

"Yeah," I agree. "Now the hard part."

We each take hold of one of the sticks that make the core of my framework idea. Leaning forward I pull with all I've got, and we take a slow, hard step. I'm panting already.

"Oh," Allie says, panting as well. "This is going to be fun."

"You think?" I ask, wiping the sweat and rain from my brow.

We lean into it again. As we pull forward it gets easier, until at last, we're moving through the jungle. Slowly. But moving at all is better than what we were accomplishing. It takes us at least four times longer to get home than it did to get to where we found him, but we make it at last.

When the vine-covered blob that is our shelter comes into view through the trees, I'm giddy with relief and a laugh slips out.

"What's so funny?" Allie asks.

"Nothing. Home," I say, shaking my head.

My heart is pounding. I'm in no kind of shape to pulling a

several-hundred-pound man through a jungle. I'm proud of myself for having made it at all.

"I'm done," Allie says as she stumbles forward and drops to her knees.

"Yeah," I agree. "Let's go get help."

As we pick our way through the trees to the compound, Rakstan emerges through the covering foliage.

"Where have you been!" he exclaims, his voice almost a growl.

Butterflies dance in my stomach but I square my shoulders and face him.

"We need help over here," I say, pointing back to where we left the Zmaj.

"Help? Are you hurt?" Rakstan leaps as he talks, wings spreading and gliding through the air.

He lands a couple of feet in front of us, looking us over for wounds.

"Not us," I say.

"Who went with you?" he asks, pushing past us. "I thought you were—"

He stops talking as soon as he sees the Zmaj on the travois. He runs over and drops to his knees next to him. He wipes the hair out of his face and cups it in both of his hands.

"Urukol?" he asks. "How can this be?"

The disbelief is clear in his voice, though I don't understand it. Seconds tick past, but I can't force words out of my mouth. This moment is strangely tender, poignant with a past I know nothing about.

"He's hurt," Allie says.

Her voice shatters the silence. Rakstan grabs Urukol up and lifts, the entire apparatus coming with him. He growls as he sets him back down. He tears at the vines we used to bind the Zmaj to the sticks. They resist his tearing and his frustration grows.

I step forward, carefully avoiding his tearing arms, then I get my hands on the main knot holding it all together. I untie it and the

Zmaj slips free, sliding down. Before he hits the ground, Rakstan has him and carries him into our home.

"Angota!" Rakstan yells.

Voices echo off the stone walls as excitement reaches a fever pitch. Everyone knows something has happened, so they crowd into the main room. I follow Rakstan and my stomach growls. Stupid time to be hungry. It's stress, I know it. That's always been my response to stress.

Angota pushes through the crowd as Rakstan lays the new Zmaj down on our dining table. Angota stops the instant he sees the newcomer.

"This can't be," he says softly, moving closer.

The shock of their recognition has left me numb. I'm thinking slow, witnessing the action around me as if it's happening to someone else. On a vid screen or something. As Angota moves next to the table, reality crashes in, and my thoughts speed up again.

This man is hurt and I'm standing around gawking. What is wrong with me? I push past Mick to the cooking station where there should be water.

"Hey!" Mick cries out.

I ignore her protest and grab the pitcher of water. It's full, thankfully. I find the rags and move through the group to the table.

"Look out," I say, forcing my way through, water sloshing in the pitcher.

I get next to the newcomer and set to work. My hands move through long practiced, familiar motions. It calms my nerves to be working, doing what I know. My moves are the result of years of training and experienced, and they don't require thought.

I clean off the mud I used to pack the wounds. His natural clotting has set in, but as I work to get the dirt and mud out, fresh bleeding occurs. He'll need stitches, a lot of them. I'm not even touching the arm yet. Every time I look at it my stomach clenches, and sympathetic pain shoots through my own arm.

One thing at a time. That's the way you deal with a trauma. Stop the bleeding then worry about the arm.

"I'm going to need thread and some kind of needle," I say, studying the long, deep wounds running down his chest.

That creature shredded him, but the cuts are clean, if deep. It shouldn't be too bad if I can close them up to stop the bleeding. The wounds don't seem to have hit anything major. His scales kept the monster's claws from going very deep, which is something to be thankful for at least.

"We don't have anything," Riley says.

"We need something," I order. "Anything."

Murmurs and low conversation rise around me, then shuffling, and people move off to search for something that will work for what I need. As I finish cleaning the last of the mud, someone lays some tools down on the table next to me. I pick them up and frown.

It's a needle... of sorts. Looks like it's from some kind of animal, a quill. Someone has made a hole through it for the thread, so its serviceable. The thread is animal gut. This isn't going to be pretty, but it should save his life. That's all I can ask.

I thread the needle and set to work. As I do, he stirs, shifting. I try to work faster, but the moving around is making it even harder.

"Hold him still," I order.

The two men jump to obey. I'm in control now. It's the first time since the crash that I feel something like myself. I hope I can hold on to this. This is me, not that scared girl who can't face the day.

I finish up the stitches, then look him over to make sure I haven't missed any open wounds. Satisfied as I can be that the immediate threat is handled, I look at the arm. My stomach flips again, and bile rises into the back of my mouth. The angle of his forearm is so wrong, it hurts to look at. There's a right angle about halfway down, and bits of bone bulging against the skin.

I have to set it but it's not going to be easy. If he wakes up...

I can't let that happen. I have no drugs, no pain killers, and no sedatives, but I have to set that arm before he comes around. There will be no way to do it once he's conscious. I close my eyes and focus on my breathing. In, out, in, out, in with calm, out with stress. A few seconds, that's how much time I give myself. Ten breaths. It's a trick I learned years ago when I was in nursing school. Okay.

"Hold him down," I order the two men standing by watching. Rakstan looks askance at me as he's already holding the Zmaj by his shoulders. I shake my head. "Tighter. This is going to hurt."

I'm staring at the arm, and they pick up on my intent, or at least they move around and get a better grip on him. I run my fingers over the arm, feeling the wrongness and visualizing what I want to do before I do it. I get a firm grip on his wrist, take a deep breath, then pull, fast and sharp.

His eyes snap open and he bellows in pain. His roar echoes off the walls, deafeningly loud, and he fights. Rakstan loses his grip holding down the arm, and a massive fist swings through the air wildly.

Angota grabs the arm before it connects with anyone or anything while Rakstan throws himself across the newcomer's chest, pinning him to the table. He talks, soft and soothingly, in his ear. Too soft for me to make out the words and too fast. I'm not fluent in their language. I know enough words to put together an understanding in a normal conversation, but I have to concentrate on it. Something I can't do right now.

I run my hands up both sides of the arm. It's not right. Close, but not close enough. If I don't get the bones aligned correctly, they'll heal wrong, crippling him further.

"I'm going to have to adjust it," I say.

"Do it," Angota says, adjusting his grip.

I gently run my hands over the break, visualizing the bones, feeling the wrongness. Once I think I've got in mind what needs to happen, I take my grip. I look at Angota, who nods, and then I jerk. The newcomer's scream is cut short when he passes out.

The arm looks better now. I exhale heavily and wipe sweat from my brow as I step back. Everyone is looking from him to me. My face warms, and prickles climb up the back of my neck.

"That did it," I say, staring at my feet. Having all eyes on me is uncomfortable. I glance up and everyone is still staring. Involuntarily I shuffle my feet and shrug. "What?"

"That was amazing," Ziva says.

"It was nothing," I counter, shaking my head.

"No, that was a hell of a lot more than nothing," Mick says. "That was... wow."

"We need to lock it in place," I say, staring at the arm. It's badly bruised where the break is, but the blood is flowing through now. The vessels are no longer pinched off by the bones, so the color is returning to normal. "I don't have any way to make a cast."

"Could we do some sticks and tie them down?" Allie asks.

"Best we can do," I agree with a nod.

We dig around the pile of wood we use for cooking and find two thick sticks that are mostly straight. Someone produces some thin strips of leather and I rig together the best brace I can. It's not perfect but it's better than nothing. I hope it's enough to get his arm to heal straight.

When it's all finished, we're left with a new Zmaj passed out on our dinner table and everyone standing around in awkward silence. The excitement is over, leaving me feeling shaky as the adrenaline drops out of my system.

Rakstan and Angota talk to each other, but they're talking too fast for me to catch more than a few words here and there. Riley keeps up with them, talking along with the two men, but the rest of us aren't fluent enough to contribute. The only thing I pick up is this man is supposed to be dead.

I don't think they mean because of his wounds either. Which doesn't make sense because he's here, obviously. While they talk, I do the only thing I can that's of any real use. I study him.

He has a strong face. I like that. It's has hard lines, a strong jaw that comes down to a solid square. It's more square than the other two Zmaj. His scales have a gorgeous light purplish tinting to the edges that gives him an almost delicate air. Not in a weak way but more of an interesting and desirable trait.

His chest rises and falls steadily as I inspect him. The old scars pull my attention. When I lean in closer, I can see they look like bite marks. They come up over his shoulder, across the lower part of his neck and down onto his chest to the top of the pec muscle. Whatever did this looks like it chewed on him, multiple marks so close together I have to study them to make out the different ones.

Shaking my head, I mentally curse whoever cared for him. They did a terrible job. Those scars didn't need to be so bad, anyone with a steady hand could have closed those wounds in such a way that the scars would be much less. I can't imagine how much that twisted skin must pain him still.

I check the stitches on the fresh wounds and feel a sense of pride in my own work. There will be scars, but they won't be as bad as the ones he has. Eventually I'm down to his tail, lying on the table between his legs. I studiously skimmed over his crotch, but I admit I noticed the bulge in his pants.

His tail is partially amputated. The end of it is gone, probably the last foot or so—it truncates in a blunt end instead of tapering to a point. More scars make it clear this was a butcher job, done with no skill or grace. This poor man was mutilated by whoever took care of him.

The other Zmaj seem to be arguing, and it's getting louder. Stopping my inspection I look up.

"What's going on?" I ask.

"They're debating if we should let him stay or not," Riley answers.

"Why wouldn't we?" I ask, heart suddenly pounding.

We can't turn him out. He's hurt. If he hadn't saved us, we'd be dead, of that there is no doubt. I can't, in good conscience, turn him out into the wet and cold without making sure he's healed first. That could be the same as sentencing him to death. I took an oath after all.

Riley shakes her head but doesn't say anything. Angota makes a sharp, cutting gesture with one hand ending with a finger pointing at the newcomer. Rakstan yells, getting into Angota's face. It's clear they're about to come to blows when Riley and Ziva step between them.

The two women talk to their men but neither man is backing down. Until he tightens his grip, I didn't realize I'd taken the newcomer's hand in mine. His hand closes startling me and then he coughs and tries to sit up.

"Lie down," I order, putting my hands on his chest and pushing him down. "You're in no shape to sit up."

I'm talking in a mix of Common and Zmaj because I don't know enough Zmaj words. I hope it's getting through to him.

Angota and Rakstan have quit arguing. When I look over, they're both staring at Urukol who's looking at them. Urukol coughs again and shakes his head.

"I should go," he says.

"No," Angota and Rakstan say as one.

They look at each other, anger flashing on their faces. Rakstan frowns then nods to Angota.

"We need to ask you questions," Angota says.

6

URUKOL

*T*he angel looms over as consciousness returns. She isn't looking at me, but her hand is in mine. My arm throbs with pain, ready to become blinding in an instant, but it's not nearly as bad as it was. Dimly I'm aware of her resetting the broken bone. Bits of it are fresh in my memory, between the blackouts.

Her soft face is round, her eyes sharp and intelligent. Her hair falls onto her shoulders in a soft cascade that I desperately want to run my fingers through. She's so... alien, yet so familiar. The softness of her skin, no scales, how strange!

Then her chest. It swells, much too far, completely foreign and exotic. I can't stop my imagination from running wild and wondering what the cloth of her shirt is hiding. My prime cock stirs but I suppress it and the urgings of my dragon. I'm not a male who is worthy of a mate. I'm a broken creature barely able to pull enough weight to warrant my own survival. I couldn't even save these two females without losing consciousness.

An emptiness aches in my core, but I don't pay attention to that. I am what I am, broken.

I'm waking up more, enough that I hear Zmaj being spoken fluently. Tightening my grip on her hand, a fleeting gesture of unexpressed desire, I turn my head to the voices. My hearts skip their next beat.

I thought they were a dream or a memory. It really is Angota and Rakstan. My brothers. Or they were, before I was expelled. Am I with the Order?

A cold knot forms in my belly, and my chest tightens. I cough and try to sit up, intending to face my doom. If the Order has me again, the Eye will not let me off with a banishment this time. I don't know how these alien females came to be with the Order, but I will meet my end on my feet. I will not die lying down, a coward.

The angel pushes me back down, ordering me to lie. The dragon rumbles at her touch and thoughts of her touching so much more flash through my mind, but they're gone as fast as they come. The situation is too serious for such dalliances.

A fresh cough causes my chest to feel like it's being ripped to pieces. The wounds pull and tear. I close my eyes and lie back, left without the strength to fight my fate. If I'm going to be killed, then so be it. I've far outlived my usefulness to the world.

"Urukol," Rakstan says my name, coming into my line of vision.

"Rakstan," I acknowledge, and he frowns.

"How are you alive?" he asks.

"Tajss wasn't done with me," I answer.

His frown deepens, and he shakes his head. Angota appears next to him.

"They told us you died of your wounds," Angota says. "Yet you're here. Do you serve the Eye? Were you put on a mission?"

"A mission?" I snort but it's cut off by a fresh round of coughing.

A metallic taste fills my mouth and my lips are wet. I wipe them with my good hand and notice that it's covered with blood. The angel is there as if summoned by my pain. She presses a damp cloth to my face and wipes away the blood. My hearts swell, pounding against my ribs. The dragon roars, urging me to take her in my arms, but I resist. That is for a real male.

"No," I say, coughing again. "I do not. I was left for dead by his minions. Still wounded, broken, then not even the decency to kill me but dumped in the jungle to be devoured by whatever happened by."

"No," Rakstan whispers, shaking his head. "Who? Who did this?"

"The Eye ordered it," I say.

"But who would carry out such an order? Who could be so—"

"Zirthoan and JKaran," Angota answers for me.

Rakstan's face contorts in rage. He raises his balled fists, and I prepare myself for a blow, trying to not flinch but unable to move or defend myself.

"It can't be," Rakstan says.

"I told you, they are evil," Angota says.

"But to leave him alone?" Rakstan yells.

Angota answers with a shrug. He's not surprised by their actions. I was, when it happened, but now it is simply a thing that happened. Rakstan shakes with rage. His mouth moves, but no words come until at last he throws his fists in the air and roars. Wordless but filled with boiling rage.

The females grouped around flinch, but no one cowers or runs. Rakstan brings himself under control, but his jaw is tight, hands balled into fists, and his tail is straight up. One of the females walks over and wraps her arms around his neck. She rises onto her toes and passionately kisses him.

I turn my head away, unable to watch the display of affection. My gaze lands on the female who has cared for me. She's looking at me and our eyes meet. My mouth is suddenly dry and my hearts race. I would do anything to keep her gaze.

My scales itch and I look away. I'm not a male. I can't protect her, provide for her, or care for her as a male should. I am not worthy. I return my attention to the two males. Slowly, I rise onto my elbows. My head is light, the room spins for a moment, but it stops. I continue to rise until I'm sitting up.

Soft hands touch my back, and I flinch when she touches the scars where my wing should be. The scar that marks me as not worthy. I hear her gasp. Closing my eyes I grit my teeth and struggle with the darkness of my thoughts. I need to get out of here. The space is too close and growing tighter. There isn't enough air in the room.

Focus. Beyond my darkness something important. What is it?

"The Order?" I ask, my voice sounds raw to my own ears. The words tear past the dryness of my mouth and throat, painful. "You're not with them?"

Angota and Rakstan exchange a look full of depth and understandings that I don't have. The current of the room changes at my question.

"No," Rakstan says.

"How?" I ask, suspicious.

Again they look at each other before either of them speaks. The others in the room, there are many of the aliens around us, now that I'm becoming aware of it, shift their weight and some clear their throats.

"Long story," Angota says. "How are you alive? How have you survived? It's been years since you… died."

Shaking my head I stare at the floor beneath my feet. "Long story." Something occurs to me then. "Are they hunting you?"

The silence and their look tells me all I need to know. I jump off the table, but the room spins as my feet hit the ground. It tilts wildly and I stumble back, gripping the edge of the table to try and stay upright.

"Woah!" my beautiful savior exclaims, her face swimming in my vision, her soft hands on my chest.

Angota and Rakstan grab my arms and lift me back onto the table. I lie down, not by choice, but because I can't stay upright anymore. My head is spinning, and my stomach is rebelling. I take a deep breath then let it out before I try to rise again. I'm pushed back down by strong hands.

"I have to leave," I say. "Have to warn them."

"Warn who?" Angota asks, suspicion in his voice.

"My friends," I say, shaking my head and struggling to sit up. "Not the Order. My friends. They're in danger."

"You can't leave like this," my savior says. "He can't travel! He needs time to heal, he lost a lot of blood."

"Right," Rakstan says.

"There is no choice!" I growl, pushing up.

Rakstan and Angota hold me down no matter how I struggle. My body isn't responding right. I'm sluggish and everything seems harder than it should be.

"Urukol," Rakstan says.

Rakstan's voice is even and measured. It is exactly as I remember him when he was my trainer. The one who pushed us every day. The one who pushed me to go on that fateful hunt.

"Stay still," Angota growls.

"Urukol, relax," Rakstan says. Lying across my chest, his voice is directly in my ear. "We will help, trust me."

"Again?" I growl, fighting to break free of their grip.

The look on his face stops me. Regret, pain, dismay dance across his face in rapid succession. My words cut him deep. He knows what I refer to, of that there is no doubt. I squeeze my eyes shut and try to shut out the memories. They're too recent, too raw, I can't handle them now.

"I'm sorry," he says, his voice barely a whisper.

His words cut through everything and I stop fighting. Letting myself collapse onto the table is a relief. Everything hurts. I'm dizzy, nauseous, and exhausted.

"I have to warn them," I say.

"Who?" Angota asks. "Who are your friends?"

I clench my jaw, refusing to answer as I think. Do I tell them? Do I trust these two males with the truth of who else is out here? It still doesn't make sense how they are out here. How do I know they're not still with the Order?

"How are you here?" I ask, locking my eyes onto Rakstan.

He won't be able to lie to me. He owes me the truth, at the very least. I also know him the best—I'll know if he isn't being honest. He looks at Angota then around the room. The female who must be his mate appears next to him, putting her arm around his waist and leaning into him. Jealousy, sharp and fast, stabs into my heart. I can't keep myself from looking at my savior, but I tear my eyes away. That's a pain I don't need right now.

"Short version, we were exiled," Rakstan says.

"Why?" I ask.

Something flashes in Rakstan's eyes, pain dances across his face as clear as the suns rising in the sky. He frowns, his hands clench into fists and his tail goes still. He opens his mouth then snaps it shut.

"The Order is evil," Angota interjects. "They Eye has lied to us all."

"What do you mean?" I ask, not looking away from Rakstan.

"These alien females," Angota says, motioning around the room, "the Eye created a plan to crash their spaceship as it passed our planet. He caused the deaths of thousands of beings."

"Why?" I ask.

"He wants to use the females—" Rakstan says, snapping off the last word making it clear there's more to be said but he isn't.

"Use them?" I ask, looking at Angota for the first time.

"Breeding," Angota fills in the final piece.

"They're... compatible?" I ask, surprised.

I know what my dragon wants but I'd not even considered it so hadn't followed the thought through before now.

"Yes," Angota says, "very."

He looks over at his female and the connection between them is so obvious a blind male could see it.

"They are hunting you, then," I say.

"We've been safe here," Angota says.

I shake my head. "For now."

"Yes," Rakstan answers. "For now. They are hunting us."

"The Eye isn't going to give up the females," I observe.

I close my eyes tight, take a deep breath, and steel my resolve. Slowly I rise to a sitting position, and this time no one stops me.

"I have to warn my friends," I say.

A loud rumble of thunder stops anyone from answering, and it's immediately followed by the sounds of a hard rain.

7

LEAH

I can't follow all the conversation, but I do understand enough, in bits and pieces, along with reading the body language. He wants to leave. My stomach drops and I want to cry. It's stupid, I'm stupid, what claim do I have to him? Why would I think he'd want to stay?

They argue back and forth in Zmaj and I try to follow along wishing I had a better knack for languages. He stands up and seems to be mostly steady on his feet. An urge hits me to throw my arms around his neck and kiss him. I don't, I'm not bold or stupid or whatever but there's an instant where I do take a step closer before I stop myself.

That would have been embarrassing. Throwing myself at some guy who isn't interested. Every time our eyes meet, he looks away. That's not a good sign now, is it? He's attractive, sure, but that's not it, is it?

These feelings for him, they're not simple lust. This is a lot more than a hey, let's jump into a bed and have some fun kind of feeling. I don't know exactly what it is, but I do know it's not that. Butterflies dance in my stomach, my heart flutters, and I want to talk to him. Learn about him. Know everything about him. More, I want him to know me. I want to share my darkest secrets with him.

How crazy is that? I don't know this guy, but I want to share my secrets with him? Obviously, I'm off my rocker.

"…warn…. Friends," he says more, but those two words I understand.

He's on his feet and looking at the door out. Neither Angota nor Rakstan are moving to stop him leaving. I yelp in surprise as a peal of thunder rumbles through the room then the sound of a down-pour comes.

"You can't leave!" I cry out.

It slips out before I can think it through. Everyone looks at me. The table looks really good right now—I could crawl under it and maybe they'll all forget I'm here. My skin crawls, cheeks flush hot, and I'm as shocked as they are by my outburst.

"Leah?" Ziva asks, a knowing smile on her face and her eyes sparkling.

Swallowing, I shake my head. One desperate look around, but no one is going to let me off of this easy. They're all waiting for my next words and the room is heavy with anticipation.

"The storm," I say, latching onto the one logical reason for my outburst. "He's badly hurt, I can't send my patient out in a storm like this."

Good lie. The best lies have an element of truth in them. The tension in the room eases, a little, enough that I can breathe again. The pressure on my chest is less. The three Zmaj look at each other then he looks at me.

His eyes land on me and with them comes a weight. I thought it was hard to breathe before, but I was wrong. That was free-wheeling and easy compared to this. My heart is in my throat, my stomach an iron knot. My lungs burn but I can't inhale. His eyes are… kind. Loving.

No, I'm projecting. They're not kind, they're eyes. Eyes can't be kind. That table is looking better and better. It's dark under there, advantage of no electric lights. Maybe they'll all forget I exist.

"Leah is right," Rakstan says. "Travel … dangerous, … wounds."

There are a lot more words he says, but I don't understand them. I gasp in desperately needed air, but no one seems to take special notice of me, thankfully. The Zmaj are debating again, rapid fire talking that I can't follow.

"Uh, guys!" Michael, the one human male survivor in our group calls out. When the Zmaj don't stop talking to listen to him, he speaks again. "GUYS!"

"What?" Riley asks.

"We got a problem," he says.

The room shifts around, and I get a good look at him for the first time. His pants are soaked and he's dripping water onto the floor.

"Why are you wet?" Mick asks.

"That's the problem," Michael says.

"Do we really need to pull this out of you one sentence at a time or are you going to actually say it?" Ziva asks, the queen of snark coming out with her frustration.

"The lower level is flooding, bad," he says.

"Okay," Mick says. "We're not staying down there so who—"

She's cut off as water rushes into the room. It's only an inch or so but enough to get all our feet wet and it's cold. Everyone cries out and people scramble around trying to find ways to get off the floor. Standing on chairs, climbing on the table, anything to get out of the cold water.

The three Zmaj are silent but also the only ones not scrabbling around like crazy people, myself included.

"Yeah, about that," Michael says.

He's climbed onto the counter next to the wall. The water keeps coming and now the level is rising.

"Shit," I exhale as I remember the water lines I was pointing out to Ziva earlier.

"Great timing Mikey!" Mick yells, throwing her hands up in the air.

"Hey, it's not my fault," he says, flinching and raising his arms protectively.

Everyone is talking at once. Yelling being a more accurate description. I'm on the table and the new Zmaj is barely a hand's width from me. I'm acutely aware of him. Goosebumps rise on my arm, his presence is so... manly. He's standing there, doing nothing untoward, but I feel his dominance, his power, his machoism.

And I like it.

A strong man, one who knows what he wants, yet in him I recognize more. It's as if I've known him before, or known him longer than I have. I feel an affinity for him that I can't explain. The only thing about it that makes sense is he's been through hard times too. He's been wounded, and he wears the scars from his wounds openly on his body. Mine are hidden, but I don't know that they're any less twisted or deep.

One wounded animal recognizing another? Is it really something as simple and as primal as that? No, I'm an evolved human. It's chemicals. Chemicals in my brain affecting my body's systems. Ignore it and it will go away. This is the effect that leads to poor choices and bad one-night stands.

And here I am thinking about all this while water is steadily rising and the room around me is freaking out. Hey, at least I'm staying calm, right? I shake my head in a desperate attempt to clear it out. We're in trouble, and I'm being stupid.

The Zmaj men talk rapid fire while Ziva and Riley contribute. Everyone else yelps, screams, and in general makes a nuisance of themselves all while the water continues to rise.

"Look, we can't stay here," I say. "I noticed earlier there is a water line and if I'm right, this entire place is going to be underwater. That's probably why it was abandoned in the first place."

"You noticed earlier?" Charlie asks, her eyes wide with disbelief.

"Yeah," I say, feeling sheepish.

"And you just now decided to tell us?" Belle asks.

"It didn't seem important," I say.

"Right, flooding deep enough to drown us all, what would be important about that?" Mick says, sarcastic as ever.

Why does she hate me? Rolling my eyes, I shrug and do the only thing I can, ignore her. She wants to hate me, fine. There's nothing I can do about it. She's going to be the way she is, and right now there are much bigger fish to fry.

"Urukol is offering to take us to his home," Riley says.

I exchange looks with the others. Fear, and relief shines on their faces and I'm sure it's mirrored on my own.

"His home?" Charlie asks.

"What does that mean?" Lisa asks.

"Well obviously it means he wants to take us away from here," Mick snaps. "Question is, do we trust him? Are we sure he's not working for the Order?"

Mick says the question that's at the forefront of my own mind and probably the others too. Can we trust him? Are we going to be turned over to the Order if we go with him? If we don't, what are we going to do? This place is going to flood, I'm sure of it, which severely limits our options.

"I trust him," I say.

His gaze shifts, and then he's looking at me. Every inch of my skin flushes warm and itches. His eyes are soft, gentle, but there's a fire burning deep inside. My mouth is dry, and my heart is palpitating. What did I just say?

"And?" Mick asks.

"Look," I say, anger overriding rationality. "You can hate me all you want. I don't care, but we don't have a lot of options, and he's giving us one. If you want to stay here and drown, then more power to you. I'm going with him!"

Shock widens her eyes, her mouth drops open, then she shakes her head.

"I don't hate you," she says, her voice soft, barely above a whisper.

If the room weren't so silent you could hear a pin drop, I probably wouldn't have heard her at all. Instantly I'm a jerk and I feel terrible. I'm the absolute worst. Great going, girl, open your mouth and make everything worse.

I want to cry. I want something to eat. I want to hide. I want someone, anyone, to say something and take all the attention off me.

"We can't," Riley says. "The storm outside is bad."

"Not safe," Rakstan says, or that's what I understand of what he said.

"We can't stay here," Ziva says, pointing at the rising water which is already up to the ankles of the Zmaj men.

Thunder rumbles again. Wind is whistling and making a roaring sound of its own, almost overriding the sound of the rain pelting the room. As if on cue a drip of water lands on my face and I yelp in surprise.

Urukol moves so fast I don't see him close the distance between us. He's there, his body touching mine, looking for a threat.

"Nothing," I say, shaking with something so much more than fear. "It was nothing."

He looks down, staring into my eyes, then he pulls back. The space is empty where he was, aching, demanding to be filled, and I wish he were still there. I can't say that, not out loud, in front of everyone, but the desire is there.

"We're going to have to make a decision," Mick says. "One way or another, if we're staying, we need to figure out a way to pump this water out."

"That's a lot of water," Michael says.

"Urukol is hurt, he's not going to be able to travel out there," I say.

"You said you were going with him," Allie says.

"I know, but listen to that," I say pointing at the roof. "That's one heck of a storm."

"Rainy season," Angota says, shrugging.

Of all of us he seems the most calm, as if this is any other day. No big deal, house is flooding, but you know, let's be cool about it.

Rakstan says something, and then the three Zmaj are debating again, talking too fast for me to follow. I pull my knees up to my chest and hug them to myself, hiding my face in them. I have nothing to contribute because I don't know. I'm not able to sort out my own feelings about any of this, much less give advice on what we should do.

"We're going," Angota says, cutting into my circling thoughts.

"We are?" I ask, looking up.

"Pack," Angota orders. "Fast."

When I slide off the table, the water is onto my calf. Yeah, this place is flooding. Great, so we're going to fight our way through one heck of a storm outside, because the other option is to stay here and drown. God, I hate this planet.

8

URUKOL

I don't know how the others are going to react, but I can't leave her here. None of them really, but if it weren't for her, would I push this hard?

Being honest with myself, no, I don't think I would. I would probably offer, but I wouldn't argue the point as I have. These males can make their own decisions after all. Except they weren't going to decide to save her.

The ache in my core is deeper than my bones. It's an ache in my soul. I wish, with all that I am, I could be worthy of her. I'm not, broken as I am, but the dragon wants her. The dragon is trying to claim her, but I can't allow it. She deserves more, better than me.

"You have space for this many?" Rakstan asks again.

"It will be tight, but enough," I say.

Tight is probably an understatement. The home that I share with my brethren is enough room for the five of us, maybe we could fit ten and still be comfortable. This many? We'll be sleeping stacked on top of each other.

What am I to do? I can't leave her, or any of them, here. This compound is going to flood. In two days it will be fully submerged as the ocean lays claim to it. No one can survive outside without shelter. They'd freeze or starve to death.

No there is no choice. We'll have to make the best of it that we can, there is no choice, I can't leave them here in this deteriorating situation. We have to return to my home.

"I don't like it," Angota says. "This is our home."

"It's flooding," Rakstan says. "We need to get these people to safety."

Angota opens this mouth to argue then his mouth snaps shut, and he shakes his head. "Fine."

"Pack. Fast," Rakstan orders.

The aliens leap into motion with impressive speed. I don't know how to help, and rather than slow them down, I step to one side and watch. In particular I watch her.

It's foolish. I'm teasing myself, imagining a future that can never be. A male takes care of his mate, provides for her. A male is a male —a whole male. I can't hunt successfully. I saved her and her friend by luck more than any skill. Wielding a lochaber is impossible because I'm too off balance.

Still, I dream. Fantasies spin out through my thoughts. Futures that could be, ones in which she could be mine. Where the calling of my dragon is answered. It knows she is mine, but why did she come into my life too late? Why not before my accident?

"Ready," the female named Riley says.

It's obvious that she is Angota's mate. I can feel the connection between them as well as see it in the soft touches and the glances. She is pretty, but she doesn't hold a candle to the one my dragon wants. No, my dragon's girl glows in my sight, like a bright fire burning and calling for me to warm myself in her gentle light.

She cared for me when I was wounded, and it's clear she did a good job. The new wounds will heal much better than my old ones. My brethren found and cared for me the best they could but none of them are skilled in the arts of medicine.

She is. A medicine woman, I could call her. A healer. When her eyes meet mine, oh so briefly, warmth floods through my chest, suffusing my scales until they itch with the desire to touch her. It takes all my will not to move to her, take her in my arms, and profess my feelings.

I'm sure that as a healer, she treats everyone the same. I am not special in her eyes. Her nature is caring, delicate, considerate of those around her. The ache in my soul throbs, but there is nothing I can do to balm it.

"You sure about this?" Angota asks, looking at Rakstan and me. "It's the height of the storm."

"I'm not positive," I say. "It will be hard, but we're too close to the coast. This place will flood and probably stay flooded for days— at least. I do not know of any other shelter close to here."

Rakstan shrugs. "We don't have many choices."

Angota looks around the room at the aliens. Aliens. My dragon laying a claim on one on sight has kept my thoughts away from the simple fact that I'm surrounded by strange beings that aren't native to this planet. Somehow, I'm not surprised. Very dimly I recall that at one point in time, many aliens visited Tajss. A time before the Devastation.

Were those aliens like these? I don't think so, but I have no clear memory to look at. A feeling, an idea, a nebulous concept is all I can muster. It makes sense, but still there's something surreal when I look at them.

They're all soft without scales, no strongly defined muscle, and no tails or wings either. I don't think they'd survive on the rest of the planet. All of the planet except this small southernmost continent is desert. Moving across the desert with their build would be difficult, if not impossible.

"Urukol," Angota says, jerking me into the moment.

"Yes?" I ask.

"This is a terrible idea. The storm is growing worse," Angota says.

He's staring at me, almost a glare. I sense his anger. The water is rising fast, and no matter how we want to argue, it's not safe here either.

"We should tie the group together," I say. "The rain will make it impossible to see. We don't want to lose anyone."

Angota opens his mouth and then snaps it shut, deciding not to say what is on his mind.

"We can use cloth," Riley says.

Angota's mate. The connection between them is palpable. The way they look at each other, the touches…. My chest tightens when I see it, and my hearts push harder as the dragon swells with its own desire. I cast a furtive glance at Leah. If only…

"Hurry," Rakstan says. "We need to move."

The females set to work as Riley talks to them in what must be their native language. It's a pretty language. The sounds of it are softer, less drawn out than Zmaj. There is a flow to it that pleases my ear, but most especially when Leah speaks. Her voice is beauty in sound, as she is in flesh. Full, embodied, rich with varied tones that caress my scales.

"Now is not the time," Angota says.

I jump. He spoke right into my ear. I was lost in my thoughts and missed him closing the distance between us. Fool. Dangerous, stupid fool.

"It's nothing," I snap back.

"I don't trust you," he says, his voice so low it's a hiss. "And now you lie to me. Do you think I am a fool?"

"No," I say, shifting so that I'm facing him. "I don't, but if you call me a liar again, we will have a problem."

Angota stiffens, his eyes narrowing as his chest puffs up. His tail rises between his wings and he leans in. I refuse to step back.

I may be broken, and I'm sure he will beat me in a fight, but I won't be called a liar. No male will impugn my honor, even if it kills me to keep it.

"Hey," Riley says, putting her hand on his chest as she slips between us. "Lot to do over here."

He turns with her but keeps his eyes locked on me. We glare at each other until he breaks off at last. My hearts thunder, the rush of blood clouding my thoughts and making me dizzy. As soon as he's not looking, I grab the table behind me to steady myself.

The cuts ache and my broken arm throbs. I close my eyes and breathe, pushing through the dizziness. Then something soft touches my bicep, trailing up to my shoulders. I don't dare breathe, I should open my eyes, but I don't want to break the moment. That touch, so delicate its intimate. It sets my scales on fire as it passes.

"Are you okay?" Leah whispers.

"Now," I say, eyes popping open against my will.

I'm afraid to look, afraid this is a dream, a fantastic imagination of me fooling myself. It's not. She's there, in front of me, a hand's width away. She takes the air from my lungs, from the room, brilliant and beautiful and deadly with her casual unawareness of her own perfection. A smile curls the corners of her lips, slowly drawing them up. Her brow wrinkles, her eyes sparkle. I notice every detail, but my attention is drawn to her lips.

Plump, full, glistening as if demanding, demanding I kiss them. I'm leaning in before I think the thought and have to stop myself. I have no right. She deserves a full male, not a broken half-male. She makes a throaty sound, almost a snort, and shakes her head.

"You're sweet," she says, not meeting my eyes.

Clever words come but I bite them off. She is kind, that is all. She has no interest in me. I return her smile but remain silent. One of the other females comes around the table and hands the end of a length of cloth to Leah who takes it and ties it around her waist. She hands the remaining length to me.

I tie it tightly around my own waist. Leah will be right behind me. Is that random chance or the hand of fate? The dragon's claim would say it is fate, but how can fate intend her for me? Now it's a cruel joke. It's hard enough, almost impossible, to keep my attention off of her. Having her so close does not make that easier.

"We are ready," Rakstan announces loudly.

He's bringing up the rear and Angota will be more or less in the middle. Everyone except me has a pack on their backs. I look around the group one final time, memorizing faces and positions.

"This will be hard," I say to Leah. "May I take your pack?"

"No," she shakes her head emphatically. "You're injured."

My jaw tightens to the point of hurting, for her words cut no matter how true they are. I can't speak so I nod and lead the way out.

Wind whistles loudly, a screeching animal daring me to face its wrath. I know how these storms are and if there were any choice, I'd never take these people out into it. Except I'm as sure that this place will flood, and staying here means they will drown.

I hold the handle to the door for a moment, bracing myself before opening. As soon as I unlatch it the wind slams against it as if it were waiting. I'm pushed back by the force and rain pelts against me.

I close my third lens to protect my eyes, but even that is not enough to see more than an arm's length ahead. Leaning into the screaming wind, I fight my way forward. The wind is shifting, hitting on the left, then the right, then it's pushing against me. The world is dark gray, wet, and intense. One foot, then another, fighting for every step.

I glance back and see Leah struggling, her feet slipping in the mud as she emerges from the door. She's small and the wind is knocking her from side to side as if she is no more than a leaf to be blown around. It doesn't stop her though, and my admiration for her blossoms in the depths of the storm. She raises an arm, shielding her eyes, leaning almost in half as she fights for every step forward. Behind her the others emerge and we're moving, so I turn my attention back to the path.

Nothing looks familiar. Internally I have a sense of the right direction to go, but there are no landmarks. I don't recognize any of the features around, and I have no idea how far we are from my home or any shelter.

Forward is the only way, though each step is a fight. Rain, leaves, dirt, and grit blast us, getting into my eyes. I pause to clear my vision. The world flashes blinding white. There is a snap. A moment of silence is broken by screams.

Instinctively, I look up. A huge black blur is falling towards me.

9

LEAH

*T*he world lights up, stopping my heart, but the cracking sound makes me scream. I'm blind and my ears are ringing. Blinking rapidly, I'm rubbing my eyes when something hits me from the side.

I want to scream, but the air rushes out from the impact. Fear takes over. I fight—punching, kicking, throwing my body one way and another. I hit the ground and there's a weight on top of me, and then I'm rolling over and over with the weight.

A heavy shape covers me, so I push against it, gasping for air. My eyes clear at last, and then I see it's Urukol, climbing off. I try to leap to my feet, but mud and wet leaves are everywhere. My feet slip out as I land and I'm falling. Urukol leaps, catching me before I hit the ground.

Time stops. I can count the rain drops hanging in the air between us. His arms curl around my body, holding me in mid-air. His face is so close we can almost kiss. I can see the pale streaks of colors in each individual scale that covers his face. A rich universe of colors that blend together to form the overall appearance of sandy tan.

It's a frozen instant then time rushes forward as it resumes, clawing back the stolen moments. Air fills my lungs and the scream I began what feels like so long ago finishes. Mine isn't the only one. Curses and screams fill the air as Urukol lowers me to my feet, holding my shoulders until he sees I'm steady on my feet. Only then does he turn and look at the others.

"Holy—" I stop myself from cursing when I see what's happened.

Rain resumes pelting us, tearing through the canopy overhead as if it doesn't exist. I shiver from the cold, and fear too. We almost died already. We've barely left our home, and this happens. Lightning hit a tree. Looking ahead, I see half of the massive tree is still standing, but the other half, more than sufficient to crush all of us, is lying on the path we've used to come to and from our home.

Urukol saved me. Saved all of us.

The other Zmaj are helping the rest of the humans. I see their mouths moving, I'm sure they're talking, but between the thunder, the pounding rain, and the ringing in my ears I can't hear them. Despite all the water around us, my mouth and throat are dry. Fear does that to me.

Urukol puts his hand on my shoulder. He says something but a crack of thunder drowns it out, so he makes hand motions instead. He wants to keep moving, which is smarter, I think. If we're going to be out here at all, standing in one place is bad, terrible even.

It takes a few moments to get everyone sorted out and to salvage the packs that were dropped. A couple of them are trapped under the downed tree. We're going to have to abandon them. Ziva is arguing with Rakstan, but I can't hear what she's saying. She motions at a pack, around at us, then puts her hand on her hip.

She shakes her head and throws her hands in the air, then we're all ready to move. I'm grateful because I'm shivering. It's really cold out here, soaking wet, rain pouring down. At least it seems to be easing up. Maybe the storm is passing.

Urukol leads the way and we all resume following. He picks his way carefully through the trees and brush. There are small trails through the jungle, barely worthy of the name. They make it possible to travel without having to cut your way through the undergrowth. Problem now is that they're mostly mud or covered in the large leaves from the trees. Those leaves are as slick as the mud, so it's a tossup which one is better.

We make progress. Slow but steady, and I'm growing hopeful that we've been through the worst of it. As if on cue, I'm knocked off my feet and thrown to the side by a gust of wind. All hell breaks loose again.

As I'm thrown to the side, Urukol whips around to help, but the wind catches his one wing and he tumbles past me. He passes me and then he disappears.

"Oh, god!" I yell.

I'm sliding along after him. I scramble, kicking and scrabbling as I try to find purchase, slipping across the mud and leaves. The cloth rope around my middle cuts into me, jerking me towards the unknown. Squinting through the rain, I can't see him.

Suddenly the pressure pulling on me stops. I lay still in the mud, rain beating down on me, eyes closed, as I take a moment to breathe. My heart is pounding, and my muscles tremble both from exertion and fear. Shaking, I sit up, letting the rain hide my tears.

"Urukol?" I yell.

The rain comes down in sheets, waves made up of drops of water washing over me. As if some great power above has decided to cleanse the planet's surface of everything that isn't nailed down. The wind blasts past, carrying my words away to nowhere.

Head down, I climb to my feet. I try to wipe my eyes clear, but I'm covered in mud and it's pointless. I yell for him again, but still don't hear an answer. With both hands I grab the rope and use it to find my way to its end.

Please be okay. Please be okay. Please be okay.

The wind hits hard, pushing back, and I slide in the mud, losing my footing and falling. I catch myself on my arms, but it's jarring.

Instead of standing up again, I crawl forward on my belly. The rope leading behind me grows tighter, then loosens.

"URUKOL!" I yell as loud as I can, resuming my crawl.

Did I hear an answer? Something? I keep crawling forward. Mud squishing, splashing up as I make my way. A shape. I see something. I belly crawl faster. The rope leading behind goes taut. I roll onto my back and jerk on it.

"Come on!" I yell. "He's close, I have to get to him!"

The rope slackens again as shapes form in the mist and rain. One is large. It has to be Angota, he was in the middle.

The rain eases up, slightly, improving visibility. My heart leaps into my throat, and I can't scream or call out for help. Adrenaline kickstarts my heart and I rise to a crouch, rushing ahead. Urukol's head floats almost disembodied as he hangs on by his one good arm.

I slide to a halt a foot in front of him and drop to my knees. He was blown off of a cliff, but his clawed hand found purchase before he fell to what would have been certain death. I grab his arm and pull, but its ineffective. He's too big.

"HELP!" I yell.

Angota appears as if he was waiting for my call. He grabs Urukol's arm, leans back to dig his feet into the mud, and then he pulls. The muscles of his arm bulge, bigger and bigger, until they look impossible.

The sound of Urukol's feet scrabbling against rock comes over the cliff, and then he slides over the edge. He climbs to his feet, shaking his head. He's covered in mud, as am I, but he's alive. I throw my arms around him without thinking.

He stiffens as soon as I do, and it's instantly awkward. I let him go, stepping back, my face burning despite the cold rain that's still falling, if not as heavy as it was. The wind has died down for the moment, and our group gathers into a circle.

Lightning flashes casting all of us in negative relief. The world is frozen for the instant of that bright white flash and somehow it looks more sinister. All of us do. Then it's gone and the thunder peals, resonating in my bones.

"We can't make it," Rakstan says.

"We must," Urukol says.

"We almost lost you. It's too dangerous," I say, looking at Riley to judge if I chose my words correctly. She doesn't correct me so they must be close enough to convey what I mean.

"I agree," Angota says. "Dangerous. Go back."

Urukol opens his mouth to argue but stops. He looks the group over and shakes his head. He says something I don't understand that Angota responds to, then it seems they're all in agreement.

"I'll lead," Rakstan says.

We switch our order around and now Urukol is in the rear with me right in front of him still. We head for home. It's a blow for sure. I saw how high those water marks were in there. Still it's better than being out in this, at least until the worst of the storm passes over. It seems like the best idea.

The storm has eased up, almost to the point I think we should keep going, but as if in answer to my thought, it rains harder and the wind picks up. We huddle closer together now. Keeping close enough to put an arm on the shoulder of the person in front of us.

My legs feel heavy. My entire body does. I don't want to keep moving. I'm tired. Cold, wet, and tired. I need a nap. Food too, my stomach grumbles in protest. I cross my arms over it and hunch my shoulders, leaning into the wind.

He stiffened when I hugged him. God, he must think I'm terrible.

Why would he think that? What did I do wrong? Besides everything, forward much? The Zmaj aren't humans. They dedicate themselves to a single mate. Forever, they say. I'm not his mate, he probably thought I was being aggressive or something. Obviously, he didn't know how to react, and just as obviously, my advances weren't welcome.

It was emotional only anyway. Relief that he wasn't dead. That's all. Nothing to do with the way he looks at me sometimes. Nope, nothing at all. I'm perfectly innocent of emotional attachments. Right.

Still, it was a strange reaction. Am I repulsive to him?

Dark thoughts flicker one to the next as a depressive spiral rolls out of control. I'm cold, wet, and miserable, so why not top it off with utter despair? And there it is. The one image that haunts me, over and over. That woman, I don't even know her name, screaming as I fail.

I failed. Why did I live, and she didn't? What justice is there in the universe?

"Hey," Allie says as I bump into her.

"Sorry," I say, looking up and out of my own head.

We're home. Wow, how long was I lost in my thoughts? We make our way inside. The water has risen but not much. We group up in the dining area, the only space big enough for all of us. The water is at my knees, but not above the tables and counters, so we all climb up on them.

"Now what?" Mick asks.

"We wait for the storm to ease up," Riley says.

"Great, sitting around, cold, wet and waiting on a storm to pass that's been raging for days," Michael says.

"You got a better idea?" Ziva asks.

"No," Michael says, hunching his shoulders and pulling his legs up to his chest. "I'm freezing, though."

"We all are, mate," Mick says. "Welcome to the club."

"Are there cookies?" Michael asks, and my stomach gurgles as if responding.

Mmmm, cookies.

"Oh yeah, double-fudge chocolate ones, extra-dark for, you know, the dark side," Mick quips.

"I'm in," Michael says.

Something creaks, loud enough that it stops the conversation. Everyone is looking around, silent, barely daring to breathe.

"Did you hear that?" Michael asks.

"You're an idiot," Mick says. "Why do you think we're all looking around?"

Michael opens his mouth when it comes again. It's a creaking sound as if something is being strained too hard. I open my mouth, wanting to say something, but then I'm falling.

The room spins, my stomach drops ahead of me, and then I slam down hard. My breath is knocked out. Can't breathe. Tears fill my eyes as I struggle to inhale and then water covers me over.

URUKOL

*S*he's so beautiful. I love watching her, though I'm doing my best to not be noticed. When she hugged me, I didn't know what to do. I wanted, so badly, to wrap my arms around her. Squeeze her tight against myself and never let her go.

But I'm broken. I know she can't be mine, so I didn't. I didn't know what to do. I don't know her customs, don't know what an embrace might mean to this alien creature. I'm sure, though, it couldn't have been a sign of affection. How could she have affection for me?

Now I study her. There's a sharp intelligence to her. She watches everyone as if she's studying them. And she's beautiful. I've never seen a more beautiful female in my life.

A loud sound echoes through the room, stopping conversation. The human male says something and one of them responds. It sounds mean, which is what I've come to associate with the female who speaks. The creak sounds again.

Leah opens her mouth, she's going to speak. I lean in, eager to hear her voice.

She disappears!

The section of the room she is in drops. The floor gives way, and she is gone in a blink.

"NO!" I scream, leaping to my feet.

I dive without thought. The water feels solid as my head hits, and debris slams against me with bruising force. The water is so deep that I can't touch the bottom. When I break above the waterline, I hear her scream.

I swim toward the sound. Desperate to find her. A female is struggling, going under the water, popping back up, sputtering, then dropping below it again. I hook my arm around her chest and pull her against my chest. She fights, kicking and flailing her arms. I swim backwards—it's hard and awkward with only one wing, but I make it work. I have to if I'm going to save her.

Torchlight flickers above. Faces are looking down into the hole. Hands reach down, and I lift the female up to them. As she rises to the light, I see it's not Leah. My stomach clenches and I thrust her up faster.

I turn and look all around. It's too dark to see clearly, but someone is splashing a wingspan to my left. I rush toward the sounds and grab the person without looking, pulling her back to the light and the opening where the floor collapsed.

Please be her. Be her. Please.

The hands reach down, and I lift this female up. In a moment, my hearts stop as cold rushes through my veins. It's not her.

"LEAH!" I roar.

Nothing. No sound but the sound of my own voice echoing back to me. She has to be under the water. This has to be a room— there can't be that much space for her. I must find her. I can't let her die.

I take a deep breath and dive. She must have gone below the water. Underneath I close my protective lenses and open my eyes. Shadowy shapes float around the water, objects that fell from above or lifted off the floor. Nothing the shape of a female. I turn, searching for her, as desperation rises.

A shape floats a distance away—it has to be her. I swim as fast as I can, reaching for her before I arrive. She must be alive. She must.

The dragon rumbles, swinging between fear and rage. My fingers brush against her arm that floats limply in the water. I pull her close and make for the surface. The water splashes as we break free and it loses its hold on us. I move her around so I can get her head next to mine, listening for her breath.

Breathe! Breathe!

I can't form words, they won't get past the lump in my throat.

"HELP!" I yell, it tears out, ripping the lump apart painfully. "HELP HER!"

Pressure builds in my head. They have to save her. She has to be okay. The fire flickers into view, hands reach down, I struggle with her limp weight, trying to keep us both afloat. She isn't reaching for them as the others did.

"Uh-cuf-uh," she coughs, shuddering.

I was trying to lift her, but now I drop and spin her around to my face. Her eyes flutter, she coughs again, and water splatters across my face. She emits a painful sound, coughs more, then sputters.

"GET HER!" I yell, pushing her back up.

The hands return, grabbing and pulling her up. My fingers trail down her legs as she's lifted away. The tips linger on her feet as I tread water and hold on to hope. She is breathing. She's okay. She will be fine. She must be. If she's not...

A chill races down my spine and my thoughts freeze. I can't think past her being gone. The cold of the water seeps past my scales, making my muscles sluggish. It's getting harder to keep myself afloat. The weight of my body is pulling down. My body is not designed for swimming.

The water rises over my head and I struggle to get above it. I gasp air. If I don't get out soon, I won't get out at all.

"Urukol!" Angota yells.

The flickering orange of a torch appears in the hole above. The water blurs the lines. I try to reach, but my arm isn't responding. It's too heavy, too hard to move. My lungs burn but my hearts are slowing. It's okay, if I saved her, that is what matters. She will carry on.

More noise. Yelling. It's distant. Is she okay? Memories of her flicker across my thoughts, frozen moments of time, and looking at each one awakens the dragon. It rages, refusing to go out like this. She needs me. Desire, need, and duty are not done yet.

My feet touch the floor, I crouch and then thrust up. My one wing is a drag, but I'm rising. I break the surface and gasp air.

"Got him," Angota says, grasping one of my forearms and pulling.

Rakstan takes my other arm and helps me over the broken edge of the floor. I fight my way over with their help.

"Is she alive?" I ask, coughing water.

"Yes," Angota says. "Thanks to you."

My muscles collapse as relief releases the tension. I lie back on the floor and breathe. My lungs hurt, burning at having taken on water. Exhaustion is heavy as I cough, trying to get the water out of my lungs.

"Where is he!" Leah yells, then she is beside me, her soft hands on my face. I rise onto my elbows, pushing towards a sitting position.

"You saved me," she says.

Her wet hair is stuck to her head, framing her face, calling all my attention to the perfect roundness. Her lips are blueish and trembling. She shivers with cold, but her eyes burn, a fire in them that shows her fighting spirit.

My treasure.

I want to say it, but I bite off the words before they can leave my mouth. Instead I nod, looking around to the others as I struggle to control myself.

"Is everyone else okay too?" I ask.

She pulls back, taking her hands off my face. Regret is a hard knot in my stomach, and I tense my jaw. I'd give anything to have her touch stay on me, forever. The itch and deep throbbing ache hits with an intensity that makes me gasp. I'm scratching at the scars before I can stop myself. Sometimes if I massage the area it eases the aching, so I force myself to do that and stop scratching. The scratching is pointless, accomplishing nothing in the end.

"It still hurts?" she asks.

I nod, unable to meet her eyes or speak again. My hearts thump in my throat.

"We can't stay here," Angota says, cutting across any further conversation. "That part of the floor is gone, the rest will probably follow."

"You want to go back out in that?" Rakstan asks.

"You want to wait around here for someone to drown?" Angota asks.

Rakstan opens his mouth, then snaps it shut and shakes his head. "Right."

I climb to my feet and then offer a hand to Leah. She takes it, and I'm acutely aware of how tiny and delicate her hand is inside of mine.

"I know it is dangerous," I say. "I do not see a choice. We must get these people to safety."

I make my word choices carefully, not because I am not concerned for the others, but their safety is a much lower priority than hers. Her presence next to me feels as if she is a warm fire, glowing and pulsing in my awareness. I could bask in her for hours without end.

Thunder rumbles, and the storm increases its fury. Going out is the last thing I want to do, and if I saw any choice at all I'd take it. Leah touches my arm, and I freeze. Slowly I turn until I'm looking at her tiny hand on my bicep. My eyes trace down the long line of her arm, up her shoulder, across her neck. In my imagination, I'm trailing kisses.

"Safer?" she asks.

It's easy to hear the suppressed fear in her voice. She's scared, with every right to be. We almost died out there, only to come back here and almost die again. There is no good choice, only less bad ones. She's looking to me for reassurance.

"Yes," I say, forcing myself to be certain.

She nods then the corners of her lips twitch until a smile breaks across her face. My breath catches and my hearts gallop, urging action. Embrace her, hold her, protect her forever.

"Urukol," Angota says, his voice almost a growl. It slices our magic moment which fades so fast I wonder if it existed. "We need to go."

He looks from me to Leah then back again, with a slight disapproving shake of his head. His eyes linger on my scars. They itch terribly in response, as doubt takes over my thoughts. I jerk forward as breath rushes in, and my hearts relapse to their normal beat.

"Yes," I agree.

Out of the corner of my vision, I see Leah frown at Angota, her brow furrowing. She looks from him to me, and then her eyes rest on my damaged side. I turn away. I can't see sympathy in her face. A mate should never have to feel sympathy for her male. What kind of protector needs sympathy?

Clearing my throat, I grab the pack I had before and head towards the door. Leah follows, holding the end of the lead out, which I take and tie around my waist. I pointedly avoid making eye contact, looking past her to watch the others tie themselves into the line.

Leah stands close. The scent of her fills my nostrils, wildflowers and delicate hints of mint. I inhale deeply until I can taste her on my tongue. My eyes drift closed as I commit this smell to my memory. Filing it with every other frozen moment I've stashed. Hidden for later, something to assuage the empty ache life will be once she finds a real mate.

Rakstan calls that they are ready, so I turn and make for the door. As I move to open it, Leah touches my arm, stopping me.

"You okay?" she asks. Her Zmaj is broken but understandable.

"Yes," I say.

The wind hits the door and it blasts open. Rain and debris break through the opening, pelting us. On instinct I whirl around, shielding Leah by putting my back to the door and opening my one wing. Wind and rain continue to blast past but it's missing her.

The rushing wind eases. I hold Leah by her arms, staring into her beautifully perfect eyes. "Okay?"

She nods. I look back the line to the other two Zmaj. They both indicate that all is fine. I steel my will before turning and leaning into the blasting wind, making my way into the storm.

11

LEAH

*T*he wind tears at us. Ripping past him, hitting me with so much force, every step forward is offset by sliding back half a step. I'm leaning so far forward that if the wind stops, I'll end up on my face in the mud.

I wrap my arms around my chest, rubbing them for what warmth I can manage. I'm freezing, have been since my swim. My drowning.

He saved me. That alone is enough to endear someone to you, but he saved me and hasn't made a move. I don't think I'm misreading him. I think he's interested, wants me, but he's doing a damn fine job of not giving off too many indicators. I'm reading between the lines, or I'm fantasizing. One or the other and I'm not sure which.

When the floor collapsed, I hit my head on the way down. I remember that much of it. The instant when my stomach dropped ahead of my body falling. The blow to my head that left me dazed. I was under the water, fighting to find my way to air, but I couldn't tell up from down.

Then everything grew dark, or darker, and I saw her. That poor, frightened woman. She wasn't my patient, so I don't know her name, but I'll never forget her face. The fear, contorting her face, her eyes and mouth impossibly wide as she screamed. Screamed and screamed for me to not let go, but my fingers hurt so much.

I tried. I tried so hard. It wasn't enough.

Shaking my head, I push those memories away, back into the box I try to keep them in. Where they'll stay until I fall asleep, when I can't do anything to hold them at bay. One foot in front of another. Every step a fight for forward progress. The wind whips around, pushing from the front, then just as fast, switching to blow from the side, and I go skidding across loose leaves and mud.

Lightning flashes and the world lights up for a second before the thunder crashes, vibrating my teeth. We keep fighting. We're going up a hill, slipping and sliding. Forward progress is minimal, if any. It seems like we're going to get somewhere, then we're sliding backwards and losing what we gained.

Urukol fights his way ahead a few feet then grabs onto a tree with one hand. He wraps the cloth rope around his forearm and pulls, tugging. I scramble, my feet slipping, arms pinwheeling as I struggle to keep upright and get to where he is.

I make it, at last, out of breath, every muscle trembling from the exertion. He repeats the action for Allie once he has me safely placed behind him.

"We can't keep on!" I yell to be heard over the wind and rain.

"Must," he says, almost growling. "Shelter."

Once Angota gets to us, he switches places with Urukol giving him a break. I stay as close to him as I can without being too obvious. He closes his eyes, head bowed, breathing heavily.

"It's getting worse!" Allie yells.

"I know!" I say.

Riley talks rapid fire to Urukol, too fast for me to follow. Damn it, I need to learn this language. I know basic words, enough to string together meaning if we go slow, but when they start rolling, it's fast. The syllables are soft, full of drawn out s sounds that drop to almost growls on some points. Listening to it at normal speed, it's kind of pretty. It has a rhythm to it, kind of like listening to a rock song.

"He says there should be a cave, not far," Riley says.

"How far?" Allie asks.

Riley shakes her head. "They don't measure space like we do, I'm not sure."

"They don't measure space like we do? What does that mean?" Allie asks.

"He said something like four hundred wingspans," Riley says.

"Of course, great!" Allie says, throwing her hands up in the air.

I understand her frustration. I want to cry. I'm so cold my teeth are chattering, I'm soaked to the bone, and it's getting darker. Dreary gray to wet black, what a change. It could be worse I suppose, we could be drowning. Been there, done that.

Rakstan arrives and Urukol pushes past us. He pauses beside me, meeting my eyes, staring.

"Okay?" he asks.

"Sure," I shrug.

He frowns, nods, then resumes walking. The trail is relatively flat, and the foliage overhead is thick, easing the rain. The wind has backed off some, so overall this isn't as bad as it was when we tried before.

No one talks as we trudge through the jungle. The wind blows and the rain pelts, making a constant white noise that is the music of our misery. Head bowed, I keep my focus on one foot in front of the other. One step closer to… whatever is coming. I'm hungry, wet, tired beyond belief, but I keep trudging.

"I don't think he knows about second breakfasts," Allie mutters.

"Huh?" I ask, glancing back.

She grins and shakes her head. "A vid I watched on the ship. *The Lord of the Rings*, seen it?"

"I don't think so," I say. "I never cared for the vids."

"You what?" she asks.

"I never did," I say, watching my feet as my face burns.

"I mean, everybody watches vids, what else do you do to pass the time?" she asks.

"I liked to draw," I say. "It's what I did mostly when I wasn't working."

"Wow," she says. "I don't think I've ever met anyone who didn't watch a lot of vids."

"I always thought they were pointless," I say, letting myself be pulled into the conversation.

"Pointless? They were fun, entertaining, that was the entire point."

"I mean," I say, trying to formulate my thoughts. "They weren't relevant to us. All the vids were made on Earth before we left."

"Sure," Allie says. "But I never saw them all, so they were new to me. They rotated the library a lot too."

"Sure," I agree. "But the content, the shows, they had nothing to do with our lives. They were probably relevant to the people who made them, but to us? We would never see any of those things they portray. No animals, no cars even, it wasn't our lives."

"No, I guess not," Allie says. "Wow, you're a bummer."

"Sorry," I say, shivering from cold. "It's only my thoughts, not a big thing."

"Sure, but now I'm not going to be able to get those thoughts out of my head," Allie says. "They'll stick with me."

"It's not like we have vids here anyway," I say.

"True," she sighs. "I miss vids."

"I miss warmth," I say, shivering so hard my teeth chatter.

Urukol stops, bringing the entire line to a halt. He's looking from side to side, his tail twitching in what I think is a nervous manner, but what do I know about Zmaj and their tails?

"What is it?" I ask.

It's quiet. Really, really quiet. The wind has stopped, the rain too. There's not a sound in the jungle, not even bugs or the calls of birds. It's an eerie quiet. A sense of being *too* quiet, if such a thing is possible.

Urukol looks past me to Angota and speaks fast. Damn I wish he'd slow down. I want to know too. The hairs on the back of my neck rise on end. Something is wrong, I'm sure of it though I have no clue what.

The two Zmaj fire words back and forth and the tone of their voices increases the sense of urgency. A sense that without direction only serves to increase my fear.

"Run," Urukol says, looking at me directly.

He turns and moves fast, his much longer legs taking full strides that count for at least two of mine in every motion. I struggle to keep up, but do my best. I'm almost at a full run. He's watching over his shoulder, and as soon as he sees I'm keeping up, he moves faster.

"What... is... it..." I pant.

"Move faster!" Riley calls out in response to something Angota says to her.

"We... are!" Allie yells.

A deep rumble rolls towards us. It may only be a sound, but I feel its approach in my bones. The hair on my arms stands up, and a strange sensation passes over my skin. The air feels electric, intense, as the sound grows louder.

I'm running, but forward progress is slow. Each step is treacherous. Wet leaves slip underfoot, and the next step my foot sinks into the mud. Urukol is looking from side to side, then back. If his head could turn a full circle, I'm sure he would.

The rumble becomes a roar, and then Urukol is flying backwards. I drop to the ground to avoid him slamming into me. Wind rips across and the sound is too loud to hear anything else. The ground jumps up and down as I roll onto my back. I'm screaming, but I can't hear the sounds. In a panic, I scrabble against the ground, but there's nowhere to go, no safety, no retreat. Lightning flashes in rapid succession. Once, twice, three times.

The trees above and the world around are cast into stark relief. Aftereffects dance across my vision. The massive trees around us are leaning, straining against the roots binding them to the earth.

These trees are dozens of feet tall, stalwart and steady, but now they're bent almost in half as the storm blasts.

I throw my arms protectively around my head and curl my legs up. There's no escape. I've never been in anything like this. I have no idea what the survival thing to do is, so I do the only thing that makes sense.

A shadow passes across the lookout crack between my arms. A shape is pressed up to me. It takes a second for me to realize it's Allie. Urukol lays his body over us. I feel the rumbling in my bones, the wind whips against us, and then there's a pelting sound.

White pellets cover the ground, rising fast, in a few minutes there is an inch-thick layer of them. The rumbling continues but the wind slows, and I can hear screaming. I'm too scared to move, barely able to breathe.

I don't know how long this goes on. It feels like forever but as fast as it hit the sound stops. The pellets, now four or five inches thick cease, and Urukol rises off of us. Allie is sobbing next to me, so I throw my arm over her and curl my body around hers.

"I... can't..." she sobs.

"You can," I say. "We got this."

Focusing all my attention on her pulls it away from my own fears. She sobs more as the sounds of the others rising to their feet surround us. After one last heaving sob, she shakes her head and rolls onto her hands and knees. I follow suit and rise to my feet as well.

"What the hell was that?" Mick asks.

"Storm," Urukol says. "Hurry. More."

"More? Are you serious?" Mick asks, shaking her head. "And you wonder why I hate this place."

Urukol bends close and looks me over, ignoring Mick. He puts his hands on either side of my face and stares into my eyes.

"Okay?" he asks.

"Yes," I say, glad I'm not sobbing.

I want to, so badly, but I have to hold it together. I'm doing my best to keep from falling apart, and I'll take the win for what it's worth. He frowns, but he straightens and walks past me. Allie is watching, face pale and eyes wide, but she has a faint smile.

"I think someone likes you," she says.

"You're crazy," I say.

"Uh-huh," she says.

The rope around my waist pulls taut which is all the excuse I need to get out of this awkward conversation I don't want to be having. We continue our trudge, but now it's getting full-on dark. I can barely see my feet, it's so gloomy.

"Shelter!" Angota yells from behind, his voice echoing around the darkness in a creepy way that makes my skin crawl.

"Almost," Urukol says.

Oddly, his voice doesn't echo, and his baritone is deep and reassuring. I have no doubts that I'm projecting, but I'll take all the comfort I can find. We trudge on. The rain falls heavier, and the temperature continues to drop until my teeth are chattering and won't stop.

It's too dark to see anything more than a few feet around myself. We're on a path of some kind and I sense more than see a drop-off to my left. We are climbing, not steep, but trending up. When Urukol stops, he turns around.

"Shelter," he says, pointing into a dark open maw. He points to me with one finger. "Wait."

He unties the cloth rope around his waist and lets it drop. Angota pushes past me, and the two men talk. Angota takes his massive weapon off his back. Its long shaft must be six feet long and three or four inches thick. The blade mounted to one end has a wicked look to it. The blade curves in a half-moon shape before coming to a gleaming point.

Angota enters the cavern first, followed by Urukol. Rakstan gathers us humans together and moves us a few feet back from the opening. He also has his weapon, they call it a loch-uh-bur or something like that, in his hands. The shaft is planted in the ground, and the blade pointed straight out from him. I assume this is a 'ready' position. I've seen how deadly they are with this weapon of theirs, and it's impressive.

We huddle tighter together, seeking what warmth we can from each other. Ziva wraps an arm around my shoulders, pulling me in tight. Allie maneuvers around until she's close, too.

"Guess what," Allie says to Ziva.

My heart flutters, she's not going to…

"What?" Ziva asks.

"Someone has an admirer," Allie says, smiling even though her teeth are chattering.

"Reaallly?" Ziva asks dragging the word out, a smile forming on her face. "That's great!"

"No," I say, shaking my head. "It's nothing."

"It's dark and all," Ziva says. "But I can still see your face is burning. It's bright red!"

Allie laughs, and I manage to find new depths of embarrassment I didn't know existed. I wave a hand around between us, ineffective, sure, and I don't know why I'm doing it. I shake my head and turn away, unable to stand their gazes, which are weighing heavily on me.

"Oh come on Lea—"

Ziva is cut off by a loud screeching sound. My blood runs cold. Rakstan spreads his wings, moving between us and the sound with his weapon held across his body. I turn in what feels like slow motion, looking towards the cave where the sound came from.

Nothing follows except quiet. I don't hear anyone even breathe. The raindrops are loud as they slam against the leaves, trees, and ground. A steady patter setting a rhythm that my heart drops into matching.

"Are th—"

"SHHH!" Riley hushes Michael, stopping him from saying more. I strain my ears for any sound. Any hint of what's happening, but nothing. The silence hurts. Pressure builds in my head. He has to be okay, both of them.

Rakstan takes a step forward, then something explodes out of the cave opening. Rakstan growls, and the rest of us scream. My ears are ringing but something is screeching and flapping. Struggling in front of us.

I'm frozen in place. Too scared to move, to breathe, even my heart has stopped. Muscles are locked in place as I stare in terror at the blackness fighting before me. Rakstan hesitates, the shaft in his hand moves up and around, the point of the blade aiming at the darkness.

He pauses, holding his position, then he's a blur. The blade whistles through the air, and a new screech tears at my ears. I cover them with both hands, screaming in pain. The screech hits a pitch that slices through my brain. It's impossible to think, I drop to my knees, begging for it to stop as tears stream down my face.

Abruptly, it's silent.

Sobbing, I look up and around. All of my fellow humans are on their knees, tentatively lowering their hands from their ears. Thankfully, I'm not the only one down here hurting. Rakstan, Angota, and Urukol stand in a huddle in front of the cave. Something large and dark lies on the ground before them.

I climb to my feet, knees shaking so much it's hard to stand. I brace myself against a tree until I'm steady, then push off and walk ahead. Angota and Urukol draw knives and begin skinning the thing they killed. Rakstan motions for us to come and leads us into the cave.

As I pass the thing my stomach ties itself into knots. A glassy green eye stares at me above a snarl-shaped mouth that's so full of teeth I couldn't begin to count them all. I know it's dead, but I still make a wide berth around it.

Inside, the cave is utter darkness, but we link hands and follow the black shape of Rakstan until we're far enough in that the rain isn't running in. We group up around him and wait for what to do next.

"Sleep here," Rakstan says, motioning around.

Great. Sleep, here, wet, cold and a hard, stone floor. A low mutter runs around the room, but then we do what we've done since the crash. We survive, doing what we must do in order to achieve that simple goal. Sleeping wet on a hard floor is by far not the worst thing we've been through.

"If we untie the clothes we used for the rope, we can have some pillows from them," Asia says.

"Good idea," Ziva says as she sets about untying the knots in hers.

We all do our parts, and it isn't long before each of us is holding a wadded-up piece of clothing and staring at each other.

"Sleep," Rakstan says, motioning with his hand. "I watch."

He motions pointing at his eyes with two fingers then outside the cave. He walks away as Angota and Urukol walk up. It's obvious I'm not the only one feeling awkward because we all stare at each other, shifting our weight, but no one moves to lie down.

"Screw it, I'm exhausted," Riley says.

She takes Angota's hand, picks a spot close to the rough wall of the cave and lies down. Angota doesn't hesitate in joining her.

"We should cuddle up," Michael says. I stare at his shadow in the dark wondering if he's being a perv or what. "For warmth!" His voice cracks. "That's all. Warmth, jeez."

"He's right," Mick says.

"I agree," Ziva says. "I'm freezing."

I don't have an argument against it, and apparently no one else does either. We move and shift around each other, picking spots as if any one place is going to be better than the other. As I lie down, somehow Urukol has managed to end up next to me. He scoots close, moves his arm across me—then stops.

"Okay?" he asks.

"Yes, please," I say, cheeks burning red hot.

His body presses against me and he drapes his arm over me. He's cool, not warm like a human, but I guess that shouldn't surprise me. Zmaj are similar to lizards in a lot of ways. I would bet, on an educated guess, that they share a lot of DNA with some native species of lizard here on Tajss. Similar to the way we humans share DNA with apes back where we came from. Science for the win.

He may not be warm, but it does feel protective. Secure, the safest I've felt in a very long time, having him pressed against me. His body is full of hard muscles and his crotch is on my ass. The instant I think of it, my lower stomach clenches tight and my pussy grows wet.

Good grief. What am I thinking? At a time like this and my thoughts turn to sex. To what end? Am I going to bring a baby into... this? We have no home, no safety, we're surviving day to day and that's it. This is no life for a baby.

But my thoughts spin out of control as he shifts and presses into my back more. Allie is in front of me and she shifts also, forcing me to press back against him more firmly. His body responds, and I can't miss it.

The hardness pressing against my ass now is a lot more than muscles. It's massive, insistent, and I'm so not ready for this. As if my thoughts weren't already going there, now I'm consumed. My nipples stiffen, rubbing painfully against the rough fabric of my shirt.

Breathe Leah, one breath, then the next. I close my eyes, squeezing them tight and try to will myself to sleep. I am exhausted and sleep hits in fitful spurts. Momentary lapses in consciousness interspersed between acute awareness of his breath on my neck. His arm across my body and his... member hard against my ass.

I jerk awake, eyes open and heart racing. It's light enough to see Allie stretching next to me. The pressure is gone from behind me, so I roll over. Urukol is up, standing at the opening of the cave talking with Angota.

I sit up and stretch, then get to my feet. Sore muscles complain. Sleeping on a cold, hard floor is rough. I stretch, raising my hands over my head. I lean from one side to the other, and then my stomach gurgles embarrassingly.

"Me too," Charlie says. "Anyone got anything to eat?"

"I've got a little bit in the pack I was carrying," Eve offers.

"Oh, great!" Belle says.

We gather around Eve as she opens her pack then hands out a single piece of smoked, dried meat to each of us. I chew on the tough meat, doing my best to be thankful I have food at all. It's not easy, but I'm trying.

"We're getting close," Riley says. "Urukol says we should be there by tonight."

"Really? That far?" I ask.

"Apparently we're going the long way," Ziva says. "That tree blocked the short path when it got hit by lightning."

"Of course it did," Mick says.

"Hey, it's not raining as hard," Lisa says. "That's good, right?"

"I'll take it," Ziva says. "This rain has been hell on my hair!"

She primps her hair, and we all laugh in response. The laughter is hollow but better than the alternative. Tears aren't far away. They're building behind my eyes, waiting to burst. Putting a good light on things is all we can do. That, and keep going.

It takes some time for us to get ready. The Zmaj insist we tie ourselves to each other, which is probably smart. It may not be raining hard right now, but we've seen how fast that can change. Once we're all bound one to another, Urukol leads the way. I'm still second behind him, which Ziva and Allie made sure of before we left.

I don't mind really, but I would also prefer to not be the center of attention. We walk in overall quiet. Everyone is focused on one foot in front of the other, leaving me too much time with my own thoughts. Only now does it hit me that I didn't dream last night. No nightmare.

This is the first time since we crashed here that I haven't woken up screaming. I'm exhausted, which is probably why. Or... I did feel safe, also for the first time. Safe and, not warm, but comforted? Something like that.

It was nice. Really nice to have Urukol there, protecting me. I study him as he leads the way. The way his muscles ripple. The scars from the hack job that was done to remove his wing pulls. I can easily imagine how much it must bother him, but he doesn't show it often. I have seen him give in to scratching the scars though.

Lightning streaks across the sky leaving dancing stars across my vision, and the thunder is so loud it rattles in my bones. It's the opening knock as the storm reacts violently. The wind picks up until I'm leaning into it to keep from falling over backwards. A heartbeat later, and the rain resumes its torrential downpour.

Everything past Urukol is blurry, wiped out by the pouring rain. He leans forward and keeps us moving ahead. The path grows narrower as a rock wall rises to my left. Soon we're walking a stone ledge with a drop-off to my right. I'm thankful for the rain because I don't want to see that drop-off. I'm ultra-aware of it. The hairs on my arms stand on end and goosebumps chase each other across my skin. Gritting my teeth, I keep from pressing myself against the wall and freezing. Barely.

My foot slips and I stumble forward. The lump in my throat is my heart, which is racing so fast I'm light-headed. I'm staring at the path beneath my feet trying to calm my heart. The stone of the path is cracked, moss covered, and the rain is making it slick. Urukol's hands are on my arms. He leans in close to be heard.

"Okay?" he yells the question.

I nod. I can't answer with words past the lump in my throat. There's a cracking sound and time slows. His eyes widen, he lets me go, then he's gone.

12

URUKOL

Her scent hasn't left my nostrils, and I never want it to. It is as sweet and wonderful as her. In my imagination I feel her warmth against my body. Last night was more than I ever thought I could have.

It's taking too long to get them to my home. The storm is a terrible time to travel, but we're making it work. Random thoughts filter through my head. If I get these people to safety, then perhaps I'd be worthy of a mate like her. My dragon rumbles its agreement to this idea. A male protects. If I can protect them all, deliver them safely, then I fulfilled the duties of a male.

The rope around my waist goes taut and I spin around in time to see her slip, stumbling forward. I close the gap between us and put my hands on her arms. Her eyes are wide and she's trembling.

"Okay?" I ask, a word I know she understands.

Tentatively she nods. I sense the next moment before it happens. My stomach drops first, and on instinct I let her go, reaching for the rope binding us. I have to release it, now!

Too late!

The ground disappears beneath my feet with a crack, and I'm falling. My one wing opens but only manages to spin me around, so

I'm falling face down. I close it, reaching for the wall. I have to get a grip on something. I can't pull her over too.

My claws scrape against the hard stone, leaving marks but finding no purchase. I scrabble, desperately trying to drive them in but to no avail. The rope goes tight, and I hear her yelp as the others scream and shout.

I'm swinging by the rope on my waist. She's leaning over the edge reaching for me. I could reach her but if I do, she'll fall too. She's not strong enough to pull my weight up and over the ledge. I can't risk it.

I fight with the tie in the rope around my waist, attempting to loosen it.

"NO!" she cries out, stretching her arm out and leaning further over the edge.

The knot will not give. I'm swaying back and forth, the smooth stone of the cliffs edge offering no purchase. There is more yelling behind her, and she turns her head to look. Rakstan appears, looking over the cliff. In his hand gleams a knife.

"Do it," I order. "Go straight on, keep going up."

He grimaces and nods as he raises the knife, preparing to slice through the cloth.

"NO!" she screams.

Rakstan doesn't hesitate, he knows what has to happen. The knife whistles as it slices through the air. I close my eyes, accepting my fate, but the impossible happens. Leah yells again and then Rakstan yells too.

I open my eyes in time to see her lift the rope from behind her and hold it up above her. The knife slices cleanly through. My weight pulls her over the edge as we fall.

We're dropping fast. She's screaming and I have the urge to scream as well but I must save her. I open my wing, causing me to go into a spin, but it slows my fall a little. The world spins around me faster and faster, but then she catches up.

I grab her and jerk her close to my chest. I snap the wing shut, wrapping it around her. Using my tail I turn us so that she is on top. I wrap my arms and legs around her, offering her all the protection my body can give.

White pain blinds me as we slam down, but then we're sinking. Water fills my nostrils and I snap my eyes open. Water.

I struggle to break the surface and get one gasp of air before the rushing water pulls us back under. We're tumbling, head over heels. I can't tell up from down.

My lungs burn, muscles ache, but I'm never letting her go.

I ram into rocks, bounce off, and continue down the river. Using one arm and my tail I try to get us to the air again. We break the surface and both of us gasp, but then we're tossed over a small waterfall.

It's a constant fight. I don't know how long it goes, but finally the rush of the water eases before we fall over another drop and land in a calm pool of water. I float on my back, keeping her on my chest, and swim for shore.

She's shivering and gulping air as she clings tight to my neck. We reach the shore and she crawls over me then collapses on the sand. I claw my way up next to her then lie face down. The rain continues to beat against us, but it doesn't matter. We survived. Somehow.

She coughs and water splutters out of her mouth. I rise to my knees, touching her face, leaning close to look at her eyes.

She coughs again, rolls to the side and exhumes more water. I gather her into my good arm and stand up. We need shelter and warmth. She is freezing cold, her body is shaking.

The sand goes for two to three strides before meeting the edge of the jungle. I scan the tree line for a minute before spotting a game trail, and I make my way to it. It will offer the most likelihood of shelter somewhere along the way.

She wraps her arms around my neck, but her grip is limp. My hearts pound, braced with fear. I have to turn sideways to enter the jungle, slipping between the trunks of two massive trees. The foliage is so thick, only a few drops of the rain reach us.

She needs warmth. A fire. My own muscles ache with the cold, feeling less responsive, and it's harder to push myself to keep moving. The dragon's roar and fire burns bright though, and that keeps me going.

I work my way through the thick underbrush and between the trees, searching for something that will serve as a shelter. Ahead there are two trees that have grown as almost one. Their trunks join together at about the height of my head. Vines wrap around the trunks, growing between the pair, making a small shelter.

I get to it and lay her down beneath it. Her eyes snap open and she clings to my arm.

"No!" she says. Her beautiful voice makes me want to do what she says instead of what is best for her. How can I make her understand?

"Safe," I say, pushing her gently down to rest.

She lies down but her eyes watch me suspiciously. I frown and try to figure out how much of my language she can understand. It doesn't matter. I have to make this shelter better and find wood to burn.

First, I gather leaves that have fallen close to hand. There are many big ones, some as big across as my chest. I gather these, piling them close to Leah. Once I think I've got enough, I weave them in between the vines over her head. It closes out the rain and provides more shelter. I keep working, tugging and pulling at the vines until I've made a roof and three walls. The job is made much harder as I have such limited use of my one arm.

As I work, I find fallen branches beneath some of the leaves which I keep in a separate pile protected by more leaves. Once I've finished the three side walls, I dig a pit at the edge of the roof.

I have no tools to work with, so I do use a strong stick, nothing deep but enough to contain the fire I intend to build. Satisfied with my pit, I pile the wood in, arranging it so the air can flow through it.

I lean close to the small pieces and belch fire. Nothing but some tendrils of smoke. I try again and this time some of the pieces of wood have the decency to smolder before puffing out and trailing smoke into the breeze.

Four more times and at last, the tinder is dried enough to catch fire. The small flames crackle as they lick hungrily at the bigger pieces. The wood is damp, making it sizzle as the flames work to dry it enough to devour.

Leah sits up, knees close to her chest, her arms wrapped around them. She's shivering and pale. Worry gnaws at my guts. When she looks up, her eyes glisten brightly. She seems so abjectly sad, and it tears at me. Pain stabs into my hearts. I want to take her pain away.

She scoots closer to the fire, and thus to me as well. I sit down and she leans against my side. I place an arm around her shoulders, and she doesn't pull away. I close my eyes and bask in this moment.

It may make me a terrible male, but I'm so happy to be this close to her, I have to allow myself a moment of enjoying it. Only a moment though.

I shift to see her better by leaning forward. A bump with a small cut in the middle is swelling on her forehead. The edges of the bump are a dark purple. She has other visible cuts and bruises too. I need to clean her wounds to make sure she doesn't get an infection.

"Wait," I say, rising to my feet.

"No!" she says, rising.

I put a hand on her shoulder and hold up my hand in front of her, open palmed, motioning down.

"Wait, please," I say. "I need to get clean water, cleanse your wounds."

She sits back down, but a deep frown is on her face. I'm sure she didn't understand all my words, but I hope she gets enough of them. I step back out into the rain. I'm instantly aware of my own pains.

The cold magnifies them after even such a short time by the warmth of the fire. I take a deep breath, then push my problems aside. Now is the time to take care of her. I pick my way through the jungle looking for a particular flower. It has a deep bell shape that will work for holding clean water. She can use it to drink and I can clean her wounds with it.

They normally open up during the storms, storing water for the dry seasons. I have to go quite a ways before I find a growth of them. It's taking too long. Longer than I want to leave her alone. The majority of predators won't be a threat, but there are some that the rains will not stop. The less time she is alone the better.

I harvest three of the hardy flowers then retrace my steps as fast as I can. The jungle is thick, and the rain makes every step treacherous. I'm constantly off balance without my wing but I've learned to cope with my disability in normal conditions. This is far from normal conditions. The ground is either mud or covered with the large, thick leaves from the canopy of the trees. With every step, I either sink to at least my ankle, or when I place my weight my foot slides, and I struggle to remain upright.

As I make my way back to her the wind picks up, whistling between the trees as it builds intensity. I must reach her and the shelter before it lets loose. The way it sounds, I'm sure we're about to have heavy, gale-force wind. I'm not sure the makeshift shelter will survive. It's also possible one of the many predators of the jungle might be driven from its shelter.

I move faster, but then my foot slides out from under me. I'm falling backwards but use my tail to catch the ground and push myself forward. I hit my head on the trunk of a tree before I catch my balance, cracking my skull.

Stars explode across my vision, leaving me momentarily blinded. The pain in my head is sharp, making it hard to concentrate or think at all. I close my eyes and focus. Leah. I summon all my memories of her, forming an idol in my thoughts. The dragon roars in my core, driving me to stake its claim.

It empowers me. Exhaustion, pain, none of that matters. She is in danger. She needs me.

I open my eyes and shift the flowers to my other hand, freeing my good arm. I run. It's not optional. She pulls me towards her. Power flows through my muscles, washes away the hurts, assuages my exhaustion.

None of that matters. I must reach her. No matter what it takes.

I'm almost back. I see the outline of the shelter I built for her. I stretch out my good arm for it, wanting to touch it, feel it, know it's real.

Something hits me from the side.

The world spins.

13

LEAH

*T*he fire helps a lot. It's small so I huddle close, almost curling around it. My front side is warm, but my backside is freezing. My eyes drift shut as the warmth eases the shivering, but I snap them back open. I can't sleep now. I'm still exposed and in danger.

I wish Urukol was here. My stomach is a tight knot that I don't think will ever let go. Focusing on him takes my mind off of it, though.

He was going to sacrifice himself for me. I saw it in his eyes. I couldn't let him go, though. I know, analytically, it's a totally different situation, but the parallels to the wreck of the ship don't escape my notice.

I couldn't save that woman. I could save him. Well no, I couldn't, but I couldn't live with losing him like that. I don't know what I was thinking when I grabbed the rope and thrust it into the path of Rakstan's dagger.

Stupid, that's what. I wasn't thinking. I was an idiot. Look where I'm at!

But I'm alive. Which is more than I think I expected. Alive and he's alive and we're going to survive this mess. Somehow.

The determination on his face as he tried to sacrifice himself. I knew, instinctively or by reading some subtle signs, he was doing it for me. He was going to throw himself to death to save me. Could I ever ask more from anyone? What am I thinking? I'd never ask that of anyone. I don't want anyone to die for me, I want him to live for me.

I think I....

No.

I can't. Can I?

Chewing my lip I let the thoughts tumble one over another as I struggle to keep my eyes open. The warmth is too nice. I'm micro-napping. Extreme exhaustion does that to a person.

The rain continues to beat down on the shelter he made, a steady pitter-patter that doesn't stop. The wind is whistling louder as it slips through the trees, but no other sounds rise above the storm.

He'll be back soon. I'm sure of it. He won't leave me alone here.

He saved me when the floor collapsed too. No one else jumped in to get me, he did. Then at the cave, he made sure he was next to me for sleeping. Maybe he likes me?

Of course he does. Don't be a fool, I'm not blind. I mean but he hasn't made any moves, hasn't said anything, he could be a lot more... obvious? Direct?

The wind is really picking up. The fire splutters, the flames bending to its will. I don't want it to go out, so I sit up and scoot around to the other side, lying down to protect the flame. My back is to the outside now, though. The hairs on the back of my neck stand on end, and a chill rushes down my spine. I can't do this. Anything could creep up on me, and I'd never see it coming.

Damn it.

The wind is blowing the rain against me too, which is making me colder. I sit up, unwilling and unable to sit with my back exposed like this. I shift to the side of the fire, blocking most of the wind, but now in a position to see outside in my peripheral vision.

Better. Safer. Yes, this will work.

I lie down again, shift around until I've got a decent vision of the outside, while still blocking the wind from the fire, mostly at least. I rest my head on my arm and stare at the coals. Inside those red and black embers, there are shapes.

I let my thoughts drift while trying to stay awake and keep a watch. I'm doing okay, I think. Something yells. I sit up ramrod straight, muscles rigidly locked. Eyes wide, I force my head to turn from side to side, trying to spot the source.

I'm too scared to blink. My eyes burn and the lids are trembling, but I force them to remain open. Vigilant. Looking. Something made that noise and it was close.

Nothing.

Nothing but rain and the wind that's graduated up to a full-fledged howl. I strain my ears and every sense. Something dangerous is out there, and if I don't find it, I'm going to die.

"Urukol?" I ask, but the wind is my only answer.

Then something growls, and I spot a direction. At the same time I scramble backwards, away from the sound. It's the direction that he left in. My hand lands on a limb that I jerk up and hold in front of myself. Some protection this offers. A piece of wood not even as thick as my arm. I might as well be holding a bouquet of flowers for all the good this is going to do.

Another growl, then a screech, and something slams against something hard. The wall on that side shakes, dirt and debris falling from the woven branches. I scream, too. I don't intend to. It slides out all on its own.

My back is against the tree on the opposite side. I've got my defensive stick in front of myself, and nothing but fear to shield myself with. I'm frozen in place. There's nowhere to go, nothing I can do but wait to see if whatever is out there comes for me.

My arms and lips are trembling, but I'm suppressing every sound. Barely daring to breathe, though I don't see how anything could hear me over the howling wind. I can barely hear anything over it and the rain pelting the ground.

The opposite wall shakes once more, and dirt falls into my eyes. I rub them quickly, desperate to clear my vision. If something is coming to get me, I want to see it coming. I think I do anyway, though I may regret it when I see it.

Now I hear sounds of a struggle. I wait, holding my breath. Quiet. Be quiet. Urukol will return soon. He'll save me. I'm not built to fight whatever is out there. I've got nothing but this stupid stick that doesn't even have a sharpened point.

The wall shakes, again and again. Something is being slammed against the tree on that side. Then at last there's a yelp. The yelp sounds desperate, final somehow. The pounding stops. I'm left with nothing but the wind, the rain, and the pounding of my heart. I hold my breath until I can't any longer and gasp air before quickly clamping my mouth shut again.

A dragging sound. Coming closer. My heart pounds faster. I'm dizzy as I tighten my grip on the stick. I'm not going to go out quietly. If I fight it off long enough Urukol might return. All I have to do is survive long enough.

The sound is closer. Closer. Then a shape forms in the pouring rain. I don't wait. Maybe if I surprise it, if I'm furious enough in my attack it will give up and go away, look for easier prey. I leap forward, stick raised over my head. I slam it down.

It cracks, loudly, and there is a yelp of pain and then a string of Zmaj that I think is cursing. The stick is ripped out of my hands, and Urukol is standing there, rubbing his head where I just whacked him.

"Oh no!" I yelp. "I'm sorry, I'm so sorry. So, so sorry."

I throw my arms around his neck and throw myself against him. I pull myself up on him and put a kiss on the bump on his head. I can't believe I hit him. What in the hell was I thinking?

He wraps his good arm around and ducks us into the shelter. He bends over, setting me onto the ground, then steps back out into the rain. He kneels, and only now do I see there's a creature lying there dead.

He pulls a knife and sets about butchering the meat with an incredible efficiency. He uses the thing's hide to lay the meat on as he slices it into long strips. I've been here long enough to know that the next thing to do will be to cook the meat, so it doesn't spoil as fast.

I scrounge up some long twigs that can be used to hold the meat over the fire and then grab some of the harvested pieces and set them to cooking.

It isn't long before the scent of cooking meat has my mouth watering. He finishes the job then drags the carcass away from our shelter. When he returns the first pieces of meat are cooked and ready for eating so I offer him one. He smiles and takes the strip as he sits down next to me.

We eat in a silence that is unexpectedly comfortable. Perhaps the good thing about not having a fully shared language is he can't berate me for hitting him over the head. I watch him out of the corner of my eye and more than once I catch him looking at me the same way.

It's such a strange situation. I'm safe, I know it, but at the same time I'm antsy. The comfort is there but boiling beneath it is an awkward sensation. That feeling that I don't quite belong, or don't deserve what I have.

He's sweet, nice, and honorable. He keeps a bit of distance which, in honesty, I wish he wouldn't. I think any human male would have made a move by now. If he were a human guy who hadn't tried to have his way with me yet, I'd be wondering what was wrong with him, or with me, but I don't feel that with him.

There's desire boiling beneath his cool exterior and every once in a while, I see it. No, with him it's something else. He's restrained, stiff even. I could be wrong. Maybe he's that way because he's not interested, at all even. What if he's looking at me out of the corner of his eye to make sure I don't hit him again? Maybe he thinks I'm crazy, dangerous even.

No, I can't be that wrong. Oh hell with it.

I scoot closer, sliding my butt across the semi-dry leaves until my hip is resting on his. He doesn't pull away, but he doesn't lean in either. That's as about as noncommittal as he could possibly be.

I get another piece of meat, tossing it between my hands until it cools enough to hold it. I chew on it absently while sorting through my thoughts. Eating with my right hand, my left rests on my leg, next to his. I could touch his leg. That would be a sign, no doubts between us that touching his leg would mean I'm open, right?

Butterflies flutter in my stomach as I nervously move my hand from my thigh to his. His leg is cool to the touch. He doesn't move but his head drops and he's staring at my hand on his leg. I wait, chewing my meat.

Nothing happening here. My hand on your leg, it's a sign, if you want it if not well it's nothing then isn't it?

No stress, nothing to worry about. I like you. I like you enough I'd be happy to kiss you, maybe more, but only if you're interested. I can't put myself out there too far.

Nothing. He doesn't react, and sure as heck doesn't make the move I'm hoping for. Slowly, I slide my hand up his thigh. Casually, not moving fast. No diving for the main event, this is still friendly, but not for much longer. Another inch or two and we're well past friendly and right into the I'm committed zone.

He stiffens and I freeze. Turning my head in slow motion, I meet his eyes. They burn, an inferno rages inside of them, they reflect the firelight, and I see my reflection outlined by the yellow flames. He wants me.

His hand moves, slowly, forward until he touches my shoulder. Yes!

His fingers close over my arm. I'm breathing quicker, face flushing, and mouth getting drier as I get wetter in places much lower.

We lean towards each other, desire creating its own gravitational pull, dragging us inexorably closer to each other. His lips part so I part mine as well. We're so close, his breath passes warm over my skin.

He blinks then pulls back. He moves my hand from his leg, grasping it in his, staring at it instead of me. Confusion swirls around me. I don't get it, we were going to…

"What?" I ask, my voice cracking.

He shakes his head. "No."

"No?" I ask, voice rising as anger rushes in to combat the confusion, fear, and disappointment.

"No…" he says words I don't understand. "Good…" more words. "not now."

"It's not going to be any safer anywhere else!" I say, voice squeaking.

He looks up and meets my eyes for a moment, but he can't hold my gaze, dropping it back down to my hand.

"Not… safety," he says.

There it is. I've made a fool of myself. He doesn't want me. God, I'm an idiot. Of course he doesn't want me, I've been projecting my own desire on to him. My lips are trembling as I pull my hand out of his.

"I'm sorry," I say, turning away.

I lie down with my back to him and the fire. I don't want him to see the tears. He says something more, but I don't bother trying to figure it out. He's made himself clear enough, and I don't need to hear anymore.

He moves closer so I squeeze my eyes shut ignoring him. I don't hear anything for a few heartbeats then he lies down behind me, close, but not too close.

My tears continue until I fall asleep.

14

URUKOL

I can't lay a claim to her. I've no right.

I don't know her kind's mating rituals, but I do know I can't commit her to me. She needs a mate who can care for her, keep her safe, and provide all she might ever need. She deserves a better man than what is left of me.

The dragon has chosen, but it must be wrong. It doesn't want to recognize that I am what I am. Broken. Incapable. It's been all I can do to keep her safe so far. Getting her back to the safety of the group is all but an insurmountable challenge.

But she wants me.

The sensation of her soft hand moving up my leg plays out over and over again. Her breathing evens out, and I'm sure she's asleep, but sleep will not come for me. I can't stop thinking about what might have happened if I hadn't stopped her. If I hadn't resisted the dragon, had let it lay my claim on her.

If she was mine and I was hers.

The softness of her curves press against me and I can't stop my prime cock from responding. It stiffens until it's aching and I long for release. She shifts in her sleep, pushing harder against me, and I jerk back unable to handle the temptation.

The rain continues to pour down and finally finds its way through the woven roof overhead. A steady dripping falls into the small fire, sizzling as the drops of rain fall to their end. Focusing on that sound calms my mind enough to sleep.

"NO!" Leah screams.

I'm ripped from sleep, bounding to my feet before my eyes are open, knife gripped tightly in my hand. I hit my head as I leap up, stopping myself in a crouch to keep from tearing through the roof of our makeshift shelter.

I look around, ready to fight anything. To protect her but there's nothing.

She sobs loudly, curling up on herself. I drop to my knees and place one hand on her shoulder. She's trembling and curls into a tighter ball.

"Okay?" I ask, one of the few words I know we share.

She doesn't answer, only continues trembling. Fear is palpable, rolling off of her. In my core the dragon rages, warmth suffuses my limbs. A male would eliminate her fear, destroy that which is causing her to feel this way.

I have no idea what to do or how to help.

She's cold, so I turn and put more wood on the fire, building it up but there is not much dry to put on. Once I've done that, I move around behind her and lie down beside her. She opens her eyes and looks into mine.

"Hold me," she says.

Her Zmaj is terrible, and I'm sure that I misunderstood her, so I hesitate. Uncertain if this is what she wants and not wanting to push her, I hold my arms out and offer them to her, but not forcing myself on her.

She rolls over and slides back against me. I wrap my arms tight around her. She shudders then the trembles ease. I bring my tail over and around, adding what warmth and comfort I can. The trembling slows then finally stops. She shifts, burying herself closer against me.

Neither of us say anything. The sounds of the rain, wind, and the fire continue and soon her breathing is even. She is asleep and I am awake. One arm under my head, I listen to her breathing and absorb her scent.

There is a hint of fruit to her smell that evokes thoughts of bright suns and open vistas. I close my eyes and let imagination carry me away on wings of sunshine and hope. The two of us living together and somehow, I manage to care for her. My brothers help us to create a home that is fitting for a female.

The home would be improved by her presence which inspires all of us to make it better. The roughness of it was suitable for males to get along in but a female should have better. She is hope of a future none of us dared dream.

A future. Something we'd all given up. The Order may have cast us out, but we know the truth. That the world was devastated, and we allowed it to happen to save the planet itself. My memory of those long-ago times is hazy but even so, I recall the pain Tajss was in. Our home, our beautiful planet was being raped of her riches. Her life blood being ripped out until she was becoming a husk of herself.

If not for the Order and the Devastation, she would be a dead planet. Ravaged by aliens and left as a rotting shell. The Order may be wrong too, but what was happening then was more wrong. We did what must be done, even knowing we were consigning ourselves to lifetimes of loneliness.

That truth was drilled into all of us. We know it, and none of us talk about it, but now? She is a female. Rakstan and Angota are mated to two of these alien females. There is hope! Hope is a delicate flower, and my imagination is fueled by it.

Can our two species have babies?

I doubt so much compatibility but in my dream house there is the laughter of children. My chest swells as the sound echoes. An electric thrill races over my scales leaving a chill itch in its passing.

Babies.

Now I know I'm drifting. How could I dare such a dream? Even if Leah were to accept me as her mate, she is much too small for a Zmaj baby. She is tiny! A Zmaj baby, as I recall, would be almost as big as her. It is not possible.

Or is it?

Life finds a way. Those words echo out of the deep fog of my memory, but something is wrong with them. They're not quite right, what was it supposed to be? I strain to recall the right wording.

Love.

Love finds a way.

Yes, that's right, but then….

No. I don't dare to be so bold. It couldn't mean, couldn't include someone like me. It doesn't matter. No matter who Leah chooses as her mate, I will be happy for her. Of this I am certain. Her happiness means more to me than any other thing in this life. Her happiness is what I intend to live for, from now on.

The fire crackles, burning lower and she snores softly in my arms. The rain eases, for now, and the wind has died to a soft breeze. I lie waiting for the suns to rise and her to wake. Traveling in the dark is too dangerous, no matter it would be easier without the storm raging. It is hard to tell how long the storm will remain docile.

She needs sleep. No matter what else comes, I'll handle it, for her. I will get her to safety. My decision is final and leaves the dragon purring in contentment. I remain awake, waiting, but I don't mind. Listening to her breath, inhaling her, absorbing her warmth, I could lie here until time is no more, perfectly happy and content.

The sky lightens slowly. It is never bright. With this being the rainy season, the cloud cover will only break for fleeting moments. The sounds of the jungle come to life as the insects, birds, and other creatures take advantage of the lull in the storm to hunt sustenance.

Our sustenance is ready and waiting for us when she wakes.

Leah shifts, groans, then stretches out. As she does so her ass presses hard into me. I move backwards, not wanting to embarrass myself or send a wrong message with my instantly rock-hard cock.

She doesn't seem to be satisfied with my response because she shoves her ass against me, hard. It had to be intentional, didn't it? She wriggles in answer to my silent question, rubbing up and down my cock.

I inhale sharply, gritting my teeth, struggling to control myself. She stops wiggling and lies still. I wait with the patience of watching a cvet for movement. My cock throbs in time with my hearts. I want her so much.

She is meant to be mine. Take her, lay my claim, she's mine forever.

No. That's the dragon. I cannot give into the temptation, unless... unless she chooses me. Freely. Is that not what she's doing? I don't know. She's an alien, what do I know of aliens and their mating rituals?

She sighs loudly, then rolls onto her back, turning her head so she is looking at me. She frowns, wrinkling her perfect brow, then a small smile forms across her lips. Her eyes light up with delight and she glows in the soft, gray light.

"Morning," she says in passable Zmaj.

"Good morning," I respond, biting off the words that try to slip out. *My treasure.*

The dragon growls but I hush it. This is not the time. I am not claiming her until I'm sure. Sure she knows what she is getting in the deal. I'm not as male as any of the others but maybe? I've cared for her so far. We're alive, fed, and sheltered even, so could I?

Her eyes drop to my throbbing erection which is bulging out the front of my pants. It cuts off my thoughts as I become acutely aware of it with her attention. Her smile widens, her lips purse, making it worse still. She bites her lower lip and my cock pulses, I barely control it from exploding its seed in my pants.

As if she knows, her eyes widen, her lips part, glistening and soft. Inviting. A delight in taste and sensation waiting for me to claim it.

No.

I can't do this. She deserves better. I'm not strong enough to give her to another male if I've claimed her. I know this to be true. I could never share her. She deserves to make her choice with all options open.

I will get her to my home. Back to the others. Then maybe... maybe she will choose me? It seems too much to ask, a dream, but one that is growing. A hope I can cling to.

My scales itch and I shift under her attention. Rising to a sitting position I motion towards the waiting food.

"Hungry?" I ask.

"Yes," she says, but her eyes never leave the bulge of my cock.

My hearts skip a beat before racing like the thundering hooves of a bivo stampede. My breath is ragged, and my cock is raging. The dragon roars seeing an invitation but is it acceptance and choice, or her own desire that will later be filled with regret?

I cannot do that to her. My body wants her. I want her, but does she choose me or is it something else? Is this a reaction to her fear? Or is it her alien customs? I don't know, and that not knowing leaves me in a state of indecision.

She sits up and turns away. The moment is gone. My cock softens, and a sinking sensation in my stomach pulls my head down with it. Staring at the dirt, I close my eyes, letting my emotions roll through.

She grabs three strips of the smoked meat and without looking at me, holds two of them out to me. I take them, gratefully, and chew the tough meat. I finish the first piece and take a bite of the second. Rain patters against the leaves of our makeshift roof, and the wind is picking up. We need to move soon before the storm gets worse again.

I climb to my feet, bowed at my waist to fit under the shelter. She looks up and her lips turn down into a frown. She tears off another bite of her meat before getting up herself. She gathers up some of the remaining meat then she looks at me.

I can't read her expression. It's either anger or resignation, or both? Her jaw is tense, her brow furrowed, but her eyes look sad. Instinctively I reach for her, but she moves her shoulder back as I do. It's slight but an unmistakable sign. Don't touch.

I understand this. I am not worthy.

The dragon rumbles as my stomach clenches tight. I nod, turn, and we walk out into the rain.

15

LEAH

*I*t's cold, wet, and I'm miserable. The wind isn't blowing hard, but it's constant, adding a chill that levels up the experience to right on the edge of unbearable. I keep slogging though because what choice is there? I can't stay here.

Urukol stays at my side, on my right. I'm doing my best to ignore him, mostly anyway. It's too embarrassing, every time I look at him my cheeks warm. I all but threw myself at him and he turned me down. Seriously, how messed up is that?

I thought if I made it clear I was willing, wanting to even, he would take it from there. His body was reacting, that's for damn sure. His hard-on was massive and felt so good pressed against my ass.

No, his body wants me, so it's a choice on his part, not an inability to perform or lack of physical interest. He's not interested in me, and now I'm a fool. A stupid, stupid fool. Ziva and Riley have talked about the Zmaj and how they mate for life. He must have his eye on one of the other girls. Or Michael? Are there gay Zmaj?

I'd feel better if that was the case. At least then I'm not losing to one of the girls. I like him. A lot. I'm trying to sort out my feelings though. I don't want to get carried away with some kind of rescuer syndrome.

It doesn't feel like that, at least it doesn't seem like it. Can I really be sure until I'm out of it? Am I ever going to be out of it? Bigger picture my entire existence on Tajss falls under rescuer syndrome. We humans don't belong here. Were never supposed to be here, but here we are.

The ground angles up as we keep moving. I slip, falling forward as wet leaves move out from under my foot. Urukol catches me with his one arm. The pressure of his grip on my arm sucks my attention to it.

I'm staring at his hand and instant fantasies fill my head of that strong grip handling my more sensitive body parts. My nipples stiffen, rubbing against the soft fabric of my blouse as my panties grow wet.

Damn it, get control! He doesn't want me.

GET. OVER. IT.

Good. Self-beratement always helps. He releases his grip, but his fingers linger against my skin which warms to their touch as my body continues reacting. I bite my lip, close my eyes, and will myself to resume walking.

My body doesn't move, but I'm trying. Move, move, move.

My heart is doing double-time, my breath is ragged, but at the same time tears swell behind my eyes. All I want is him to want me too. I don't want to be alone anymore. My throat clenches, my mouth is dry, and I can't speak, can't move, can't do anything but stand here suffering.

Riley has Angota, Ziva has her man, if I had a man, one who looks at me like their mates look at them, then the fear would stop. How could I be scared when a man loves you the way theirs obviously love them? No human man can possibly compare to the devotion of a Zmaj. Their woman is an altar that they worship at with a fervor I've never seen.

I want to feel that much love.

Almost, I do. Like right now. His fingers are still touching my arm, as if he doesn't want to break this simple, platonic contact any more than I want him to.

Don't stop, more. Touch more, touch all of me.

Thunder rumbles so loud it shakes my bones and I snap my eyes open, squealing in surprise and fear. I jump and before I land Urukol has his arms wrapped around me. His one wing folds around us, sheltering me and stopping the rain, if only for a short time. I wrap my arms around him.

Don't be clingy. He doesn't want me. It's fine. Take comfort, move on.

I try. I really, really try, but he feels so good. His scales aren't rough but smooth. His chest is cool against my face, offsetting the burn in my cheeks.

I'm clinging. Let go.

My arms don't loosen. Probably because I don't want to let him go. I want to hold him tighter, meld into him. He doesn't push me away. If anything, he tightens his grip. I don't know how long we stand here, accomplishing nothing but teasing each other, but at last my arms obey my commands and ease their death grip.

As I loosen my grip, he follows suit and finally I take a step back. He closes his wing drawing my eyes to his scars and the makeshift cast I put on his arm. The way the scars pull with the motion of his wing must hurt. Those scars are twisted, angry, very rough. A butcher job if ever I saw one.

He may be broken, but he's still powerful and beautiful. The scars add flavor, give him an air of having been through it and come out the other side. He's a survivor. I've spent my life helping those who've had the worst day of their lives. Pilots who were caught in the flaming wreckage of their planes. Training accidents that left the person mauled, burned, or torn in ways that no one's body should ever be put through.

I know scars. I know pain. In caring for others, I've always been able to hide my own. He's different though. I don't feel for him the way I have for so many others. It's not empathy. It's deeper. Richer. Filled with colors that I didn't know existed in the world.

He has saved me so many times, but even that isn't enough to satisfy the way I feel. The depth of this is so much more. I touch his chest, trailing my fingers across the bulging pectoral muscles down to the top of his rock-hard abs.

Every Zmaj I've met looks like they should be on the cover of a romance novel or a body-builder poster. Bulging muscles on full display since they don't wear shirts. He's always cool to the touch, in a pleasing way. The color on the edges of his scales shifts. It's subtle, and if I weren't studying him so closely, I'd probably have missed it, but seeing it, I can't unsee it. Interesting.

"Okay?" he asks, breaking into my careful study.

"Huh? Yes," I nod probably with too much enthusiasm as I try to cover over how flustered I am. "Yes."

"Good," he says. He cups his hand under my chin and gently pulls my eyes up to meet his. "Care."

He pats his chest and repeats the word. I'm translating it but I'm certain I get what he means. He cares. About me. Oh...

The mix of crazy emotions paralyzes me. Can't breathe. Can't think. Smile? No? Frown? Nod? Grin like a fool? Yeah, that's the one, I'll do that.

Oh, what am I doing? I stop the stupid grin, grabbing control of myself and make it a simple smile.

"Thank you," I say, earnestness making my voice heavy, but I'm in control here. I am a big girl, got this all day long. I motion, placing a hand on my chest then placing it on his. "Me too."

Emotions race across his face. He'd be a terrible poker player except I can't read them clearly because there seem to be so many that his face is a storm of conflicting possibilities. Which possibility is reality though?

I pull my hand back, uncertain and afraid to push. No, the next move is his. I made my move and he turned me down. Ball is firmly in his court. His tail shifts, curling around his leg and touching mine. A shiver races up my leg, and I bite my lip to keep myself under control. I'd never, in all my days, have thought a tail could be sexy, but damn he pulls it off.

He clears his throat as the air between us vibrates with the tension between the two of us. Please take me. No, wait, what is wrong with me? He turns and resumes walking. The tension eases as we progress forward. It's there, but not at the forefront of everything at least. That's better, I think.

Thunder rumbles and then the rain becomes an instantaneous downpour. Water runs in tiny wannabe rivers past our feet, racing down the incline. It's coming down so hard I can barely see Urukol walking beside me.

I hold out my hand then realize I'm on the side with his broken arm. I touch his arm as I step behind him and switch sides. When his hand closes on mine, gratitude swells in my chest. It's safe, he'll protect me.

Heads down, we walk against the driving rain. It's so cold I'm shivering, but the wind keeps blowing harder. Each rain drop hits harder and harder as the wind picks up. I'm leaning into the wind to keep myself upright. He lets go of my hand to move his arm behind the small of my back, helping me to stay up.

My feet become my entire world. One foot forward, then the next. Hours pass, or it feels like hours. There's nothing to measure time against except forward motion. Step, shiver, step, rub arms, step, squint against the wind and rain, step.

Over and over. Unending. My thighs throb, my stomach clenches, and I'm huffing each breath. The world is wet and gray. The wind blows harder and harder until now leaves are hitting, lifting off the ground and slapping my face.

I raise an arm to protect my face as a gust blasts us. Debris comes in fast, so I turn my back to it. Urukol steps behind me, placing himself between the assault and my body, protecting me. Tears stream down my face, but the rain hides them. This is awful.

We can't make it, can't go on like this. I'm sobbing and can't stop myself.

Urukol wraps his arm around and pulls me against him. The wind whistles past, accented by the sound of debris hitting his back. I thought life was hell before, but this is worse. Impulsively I wrap my arms around him, clinging to his strength. He's a rock in this storm, the one solid thing.

The wind keeps blowing harder and harder. He's swaying with the force of it. I keep my eyes squeezed shut as my arms squeeze him tighter with a will of their own.

"Must. Move," he yells to be heard, and even so, I barely hear his words.

I nod without bothering to speak. He doesn't let me go, but takes a step to the left. I follow his lead, moving with him. We reach one of the massive trees, and he gets us behind its protection, which doesn't turn out to be much. The wind seems to have taken the shelter the tree offers as a challenge, blowing harder still.

I'm blasted from side to side as the wind splits around the tree only to slam into me. Urukol keeps a firm grip as he turns us, smashing me between himself and the tree. The wind howls, and it's a terrifying sound that makes my heart race.

I'm shaking uncontrollably. Cold and fear make a powerful combo, leaving me a quivering mess. We're never going to escape. This is never going to end. We're lost, and hope is being blown away along with all the loose debris from the jungle.

"Urukol!" I yell, but the wind whips my words away.

I don't think he can hear me. He's clinging to the tree with his one good hand, but the wind is buffeting him and me. We can't stay here, it's growing more dangerous by the minute. The trees are shaking violently. Smaller ones fall with silent crashes, the sound drowned out by the roaring wind.

Urukol looks down, our eyes lock for an instant. His brow furrows, frowning he shakes his head. I'd think it impossible, but the wind is stronger. Bigger trees fall around us, slamming to the ground, driving more debris into the air.

I close my eyes tight and cling to Urukol. I'm sure we're going to die. The wind slams into my left, shifts in the blink of an eye, and slams into my right. Urukol is knocked back and forth. We're so screwed.

I hope the others are safe.

Without warning we're tumbling. My stomach rebels, sickness rising in my throat, but I fight it down. Desperate, I cling to Urukol with all the strength I can summon. His one arm is so tight, it feels I'm about to be squeezed in half.

I keep my eyes shut. I don't want to see what's next. Urukol slams against something so hard it rattles my bones. We barely slow down with the hit and we're tumbling again. I hit the ground, and then we roll and fly through the air only to slam to earth again.

The wind blows us across the slick ground. I open my eyes in time to wish I hadn't seen what's coming. We're heading for a drop-off, and as fast as I realize what's happening, we go over the edge.

My stomach is left far behind. Tumbling in free fall, I'm sure this is it. I'm suffused with a sense of acceptance and I relax. I've survived so much, it's only fitting I end like this. Perhaps this is what my nightmares have been telling me. A warning of what was to come, not a revivification of the past.

It wasn't my failing to save that unknown lady, it was a sign that I would end the same way. Falling into an endless black. I'm not going to open my eyes, it's okay. Urukol did his best, he kept me alive longer than I would have made it on my own.

My only regret is not getting to know him better. I think we could have been something. Maybe. I'd like to have had the option at least.

Black.

White pain.

Blinding.

Can't breathe.

Something blocking nose.

Open mouth and liquid pours in. Try to scream, can't.

I snap my eyes open and fight. Air. Have to have air. Must breathe.

Can't move fast. World resists, not giving up.

I break free and delicious, humid air fills my lungs in a rush of relief so great I cry. It's the hardest rain I've been in yet but I'm treading water. Turning my head it hits me we're in a lake or pond or something.

Not we.

I am.

"URUKOL!" I scream his name, voice cracking, throat burning.

Nothing. The whistle of the wind and waves peaking over my head, water up my nose. I bend and dive, opening my eyes under the water. It's too murky to see. He has to be close. I grasp blindly through the water.

He has to be okay. Has to be. I can't survive this if he doesn't. Fate can't be that damn cruel. Please, I beg. My lungs burn so I swim up, gasp in air, and dive again.

Kicking around, swimming blindly as I push my hands around the dirty water. My fingers brush something that feels like scales. I grasp, but it twists oddly in my hand, and something primal in my brain fires off an alarm.

I let it go and break for the surface, screaming the moment air hits my lips. The water around me froths violently. I blink rapidly to clear my eyes, and a large shape bursts out of the water then rolls and dives back below.

"Urukol!" I scream.

Once more the shape comes up from the depths and this time, I see it is him—but he's not alone. A snake-like thing has him wrapped in its coils.

He roars. One arm is free, gripping the hissing monster right below its head, holding it at bay. Its mouth is wide open, exposing four massive fangs and a flickering tongue.

I have to help him, but how?

They dive back beneath the water. The frothing slows then stops. Oh god. Is he?

No. He has to be okay. Have to help him. Desperate, I look around again for anything that will be helpful. The shore is a short distance away, but there's nothing there of use. Swimming a circle, I keep looking. There's a cliff and a waterfall roaring over it, that must be where we came from, up there.

It's impossibly far up. Scarily far up. Tearing my gaze away from it, I finish my circle, but nothing. There has to be something I can do.

A loud splash and the two of them break the surface again. Urukol gasps air, growling as he fights the thing.

His knife. He doesn't have his knife. A glimmer of hope but it's all I've got. Inhaling deeply, I dive deep, swimming down. Please, please don't be too deep. Waving my arms in front of myself I swim and feel my way down. I'm so thankful when my hands touch mud.

The water here is less cloudy, which aids my search. Something glints off to my right. I swim that way feeling the life or death struggle happening over my head.

I'm almost to it. Lungs burning I push myself to reach what I saw, and luck is smiling. His blade is sticking up out of the mud. I grasp the hilt and push off the bottom as I break for the surface.

Air fills my lungs tasting sweeter than honey. Urukol and the monster break the surface a heartbeat after I do. Its coils are wrapped around most of his body, and it's clear he's losing the fight.

I swim towards them before the primal part of my brain can tell me to stop my intended insanity. Arm over arm I swim, kicking my feet and closing the distance. They're rolling over and over, and I pause an arm's length short.

They roll again, and I'm ready. I slash with the knife.

It slides across the thing's scales without leaving a mark.

"No," I say, shaking my head.

That's not what was supposed to happen. It should be cut, bleeding, letting him go. They disappear under the surface again. Will this be the last time? Can Urukol keep fighting it?

I count my heart beats. One, two, four, six, nothing. They're not back up. Damn it.

I dive knowing that it's now or never. Knife held in one hand with my grip so tight it hurts I open my eyes and squint looking for them. When I spot them my heart races. Urukol is barely fighting. He's close to the end but not dead yet.

He's mine you slithering son of a bitch.

Kicking my legs I move close, turning the knife in my hand. Cutting it didn't work so I'm going to stab the damn thing.

Urukol's grip below its head offers the best target. The head is far enough away from him that I should be able to hit it without fear of stabbing into him. Urukol sees my approach. Shakes his head and fights with renewed strength.

I line up, carefully aiming my thrust. I can't screw this up. I tense my arms, grit my teeth, and then drive the knife up. The water slows the motion, but my aim is true. The point of the blade slides into the beast's flesh, up and through until the knife emerges from the top of its head. It convulses, Urukol growls, and then it gives one last, violent thrashing before its coils loosen and it slides off him and drops below the water.

Urukol gulps air then reaches for me. His eyes are wide as he looks me over. He bobs up and down, barely keeping his head above water with only one good arm. Zmaj aren't well designed for water.

"Shore," I say, pointing in hopes it will help him understand what I mean.

He nods and we swim towards shore, staying next to each other. My arms tremble with the exertion, and my entire body aches, but I push through. The water becomes shallower until I can stand up. It's freezing. Wrapping my arms around myself, I stumble out of the water and collapse on the sand.

Urukol moves closer. I'm shivering so hard my teeth are chattering. He touches my face, leaning in so close he could kiss me. His body lies on mine, heavy, but not offering much in the way of warmth.

His fingers trail across my cheek, and my body responds to his touch, or wants to, but I'm too cold. The rain pouring down is cold, the wind has a chill, and I'd give anything to be warm. Urukol climbs up to his knees and hooks his one arm under my middle. I wrap my arms around his neck to help and he stands the rest of the way up.

He rushes across the small beach to the trees. They cut the wind some, which helps, but my teeth are still chattering. He sets me down in the crook of a large tree. The massive roots rise high enough to redirect the worst of the wind over us. He touches my face again, shifts me around with his one arm, then leans in close.

"Okay?" he asks.

"C-c-c-o-l-d-d," I say.

He stands up. "Wait."

He disappears, leaving me to curl in on myself, rub my arms, and try to generate any amount of warmth I can. This is just shock, the analyzing part of my mind says, not that it helps knowing it. It certainly doesn't make me warm.

Rain drips onto my head and runs into my eyes. It's too much effort to wipe them so I close them instead. The wind blows, splitting around the tree, whistling as it races past. Something thuds close and I snap my eyes open. Urukol is back, his broken arm stacked with pieces of limbs and debris.

He kneels in front of me and works to build a fire. It takes a long, miserable time. He's breathing fire not to start a better one, but to dry out the material so he can. When the first sputtering flames catch, I'm more excited than when I was a kid at Christmas.

I lean in, huddling over the small fire while Urukol works to build it into something more substantial. He adds small pieces of wood to it, one at a time, until at last there is sufficient fire to warm me.

The warmth soaks into my face, so I hold my hands over it, turning them until they too are warm. Urukol sits beside me and puts his good arm around my waist. I rest my head on his shoulder and close my eyes.

The cold of his scales seeps into my cheek, and I realize due to his nature he must be colder than I am, but he's been hiding it. I shift towards him and rub my hands up and down his arms and up across his shoulders.

As my hands reach his face, my core tightens. There is one sure way to warm us, and he looks so damn good. His hair is pasted to his head, random strands hanging down across his forehead. I climb onto his lap, pressing my breasts against his chest, and run my fingers through his wet hair.

I like the texture of it, soft but thick with soft curls that wrap around his small horns. His horns are not big like some of the men, little nubs that protrude from right past his hairline. He closes his eyes and lifts his head emitting a soft moan.

I wrap my legs around his waist, and his massive erection presses hard against my pussy that is wet from a lot more than the rain. I groan as desire reaches a peak.

He runs his arms up and down my back, leaning his head back and parts his lips. He doesn't push forward, giving control to me.

I take it.

He's mine. I want him more than I've ever wanted a man.

I wrap my hands in his hair and jerk his head to mine. Our teeth click but then his soft lips meld with mine. I drive my tongue into his mouth, seeking his.

I grind my hips, his hard cock teasing my clit, and he groans into my mouth. The cold isn't a problem any longer—he's hot and I'm burning.

He grips my ass, jerking me against him. I fall into him without breaking the kiss until my pussy spasms and I gasp. He thrusts up and down with his hips. His cock feels massive and rock hard rubbing against me.

I kiss his forehead and up to his small horns while he kisses my neck and down the opening of my blouse.

I want his mouth on my tits. I lean back, causing my pussy to rub harder, grabbing at the restraining buttons. I barely stop myself from ripping the shirt open. I don't have another and that would be stupid.

The buttons resist. "Damn it."

I fumble with them then Urukol places his hands over mine.

"Help," he says.

Feeling reluctant I pull my hands away and let him do it. He's gentle, controlled, unfastening each button with a determined care. I'm breathing fast, my chest rising and falling, my tits pushing trying to break free long before he has undone enough buttons.

All my attention is on the slow, delicate process. Enthralled by the care he gives to each one. His eyes studying my skin as each button exposes more. The concentration of his face is as if he's committing every goose-bump of my chilled skin to memory.

His intensity in this simple act is sexy, but so much more. It's him, the way he gives his full attention to each motion. Taking care that each one is exactly right. It's a devotion, not only to undoing my buttons, no. To me. He's devoting himself and this moment to me.

My heart skips and my throat clenches tight, causing me to gasp. He pauses, looking up, and when our eyes meet, the love in his envelopes me. This is so much more than sex.

"Treasure," he whispers, and I shiver.

I grasp his face between my hands and kiss him. A kiss deeper than any I've given or received in all my life. I run my hands down his neck, over his shoulders, pausing when my hand reaches the twisted scar tissue. He flinches, it's subtle but unmistakable.

I break the kiss and he averts his eyes. He's ashamed but has no reason for it. I kiss his neck then I softly kiss my way across the scars that mar his shoulder and drop onto his chest. He gulps air, his cock pulsing between us.

I drop my free hand down and slide it under his pants, seeking his hard member. I pause as my fingers touch it for the first time. It's strange feeling, I can't figure it out, my mind won't form a picture of why it feels so different.

There's nothing for it but to see. I want to see his cock, taste his cock, feel it inside me.

I scoot back along his legs to free up space to loosen his pants and see it. As the loose cloth all the Zmaj wear for pants falls down, his impressive erection rises on display. I bite my lip.

It's huge, but not unmanageable. That's not the part that gives me pause. It's... ribbed. Up and down the top side there are bone ridges, and at its base, as if designed specifically for a human female, there's a... nub. It takes no imagination to know it will rub my clit if I am able to fit the entire thing inside.

I'm staring but my mouth is open. The pulsing purple head glistens with his excitement. I shift further back and bend over, tasting him for the first time. He's salty but sweet, inviting.

His cock thrums as my tongue touches it, so I trail my way down the underside. The underside is soft, like any human cock. I close my lips around that part and move my way up and down. He groans loudly, thrusting his hips up.

He runs his hands through my hair while I pleasure him. I undo my own pants while I work and drive my fingers into my wet pussy.

When his cock is pulsing so hard I'm sure he's about to cum, I stop. I sit back onto his lap and now I'm teasing.

I undo the last three buttons of my blouse. He's a frozen tableau, watching with bated breath as I unveil myself. His tongue darts out, licking his lips.

My shirt falls to either side, revealing my full, but not large breasts. Reaching behind myself, I undo my bra. His eyes never leave my tits. It's as if he's never seen a pair before.

I slide my bra off, and they drop with a soft bounce that his eyes follow. He leans closer, slowly, glancing up as if he expects me to stop him. I push my chest towards him, this is part of what I've been waiting for.

When his mouth closes on my nipple, I scream in pleasure. Grabbing his head, I jerk him back onto them when he tries to stop.

"MORE!" I yell.

His tongue bathes the nipple, and he does something that I can't define, but the sensation is incredible. I'm lost in the pleasure, bucking my partially exposed pussy against his full exposed cock.

He moves from one breast to the other and back in rapid succession. Almost expertly he keeps both nipples rock hard. Each one aches while he's on the other then he rolls it between his thumb and forefinger.

I grab his cock and pull it towards my clit, leaning back enough that I can rub up and down his shaft. It's more than I can stand. I lock into the struggle with my pending orgasm. Fighting to hold it at bay as long as possible, until it builds to the point I can't hold off any longer.

My back arches, toes curl, and I lean my head back, crying out my pleasure.

His one good arm holds me up as my body is wracked by wave after wave of pleasure. At last I collapse against him, burying my face in his shoulder. I'm panting as the aftershocks pass through one after another until I'm left empty.

I kiss his scars, up his neck, until I find his mouth again.

His cock has left a mess between us but neither of us care. It softens in my hand, dropping away but something stirs.

I shift on his lap and my mouth drops open as my eyes widen. A second cock rises, every bit as big, and as hard as the other was.

"Two?" I ask, smiling.

He shakes his head, not understanding the word, and I don't know how to say it in Zmaj. He looks down then back up, frowning.

"Not okay?" he asks.

"Better than okay," I say, warmth suffusing my lady bits.

Two. I guess the rumors were true but Ziva and Riley could have been more open about this. One way or another, hell yes, I'm in.

I stand up and slide my pants out of the way. Before I move to sit on his new cock, he touches my thigh and shakes his head. I frown, covering myself with my arms but feeling very self-conscious.

He stares, moving his eyes from the top of my head and slowly down. It takes me a moment to warm to it but the look on his face is one of such devotion and admiration I move my arms away and display myself for him.

His mouth opens, and I can feel the love rolling off of him. I've never felt anything such as this before. It's waves of emotion, respect, it's love. I don't have words more than that. His love is a palpable thing washing across me like the sheets of rain pouring down from the sky.

As my comfort rises, I lift my hair, shift my weight from foot to foot, and show myself off to him. He grabs his hard cock and slowly strokes it, encouraging my display.

I run my hands down my face, neck, along my tits, and down onto my thighs. As I bring them back up again, I pass one hand over my pussy and open my delicate lips to his inspection. He responds by gulping air and stroking faster.

I turn in a slow circle, gyrating my hips. When my ass is to him, I bend over, running my hands down my thighs. He groans. I look back to him as I shake my ass. He rises onto his knees, keeping his good hand on his cock, and moves close.

He kisses my ass, up to my spine, down the other cheek. I close my eyes, enjoying his rough tongue as he moves it around my skin.

He takes his good hand and slides it between my thighs. When he reaches my pussy, he rubs the outside until his fingers are wet, then he slides two of them inside.

I gasp as I'm filled.

He pushes them in and out while continuing to kiss around my back and ass, down onto my thighs, and all around. He doesn't stop, pushing so hard I'm swaying, forcing me to spread my legs to keep my balance.

I bite my lip, pushing back against his hand. He doesn't stop his thrusting. A fresh orgasm is building fast.

"Inside," I groan. "Fuck me. Please."

I'm not speaking in Zmaj, have no clue what the words I need are, but he gets my point. He pulls his hand out, leaving me feeling empty.

He climbs to his feet, and bending his knees, presses the hard head of his cock to my opening. He slides it in so slow, it's hardly better than the tease building it up. I groan as the first hard ridge presses against me.

He hesitates, and I sense more than anything he's afraid of hurting me. My needs won't wait for his concerns.

I push back, hard. His cock bursts into my pussy as if he's kicking in the door. I cry out, but it's cries of pleasure.

Nothing has ever felt this good. It's beyond words.

I'm panting, heart racing, pussy throbbing as muscles clench and relax around his cock without either of us making a motion.

I swear I'm going to cum without a further action.

He grabs my hip, steadying me the best he can. As the exploding pleasure centers adjust to their new normal, I slide forward.

His cock emerges from me one ridge at a time. I'm bent in half, watching it come out. I can't believe it all went in so fast and easily. More, I can't believe how good it feels.

Once only the head remains inside, I inhale deeply and thrust back. My pussy takes it like a champ, devouring his cock and ready for more.

Now he's gasping, panting, and together we find a rhythm.

A rhythm of each other as we join again and again. Each thrust in is a coming together, each retreat is an erasure of barriers.

Fears dissolve because this sex is creating a new reality. It's not sex, it's love. Sensations rush through my body that go beyond pleasure.

He doesn't fuck me, he loves me. He gives himself to me so deeply, so thoroughly, I'm left weak, exposed. He doesn't hold back. Nothing, it's all mine, to take or to leave.

He drives his love in and jerks away the layers of protection. Barriers I didn't know I had are being smashed until there is nothing but me. Me and him.

Me, him, and a choice.

Do I give myself to him or not?

How can I not?

He is everything I've ever dreamed of having in a mate. Dreams I didn't know I even had, the imaginings of a lifetime that you keep hidden away because on some level you know they're not real. They can never be, yet here he is.

In me.

Giving to me.

Over and over, baring his soul.

And I can do no less.

Reaching back I find his hand and grasp it in mine as we move together and not a moment too soon. He thrusts hard, growling, and I scream as a second orgasm wracks its way through my body.

His cock spasms and bursts, his seed pumping into me as if a dam has broken. Flooding my pussy as we both are gripped by our pleasure.

My knees are shaking. I rise up, his cock still inside, and he wraps his arm around my middle under my breasts. I lean my head back so we can kiss while the aftermath of the orgasms continue to clench my body.

At last his dick softens, and we're holding each other. The cold wind causes us both to shiver, cutting into the tender moment.

"Dress," I say, motioning towards my piled clothes.

He gets my meaning, bending his knees to pull his soft cock out, and we dress for warmth. The rain is only a drizzle, barely making it past the canopy of the jungle. We sit next to the small fire, cuddling together.

Resting my head on his chest, listening to his heart echo in my ears I'm safe. It's a sensation I don't think I've felt since before the crash. A little thing that I took for granted in my life on the ship.

On the ship I never feared for my life. Life was controlled, planned. Sure things happened. I saw people quite often on the worst day of their lives when I'd do a rotation in the emergency room. Accidents, unplanned events leaving someone injured. That's life, and never once did it leave me feeling like I've been on this planet.

Fear has been my constant companion for so long now, I'd forgotten what it felt like to not be scared. Until now. Until him.

"When the ship wrecked," I say, mixing in my smattering of Zmaj words, hoping he'll get the gist of what I'm saying. "I was scared. So, so scared."

I shake my head against him, shivering as the memory evokes my old friend fear. He doesn't say anything, but he's listening attentively, running his fingers through my hair.

"I was on duty," I continue, tears filling my eyes, "when the attack happened. I'm a nurse, you see. I care for hurt or sick people. It was my second shift in a row. Julia, the girl who's shift it was supposed to be, had called in, and we were short-handed. It wasn't my normal floor. I didn't know the patients like I would my own, but they needed care. Then the attack happened..."

I trail off, choking up and unable to keep talking.

Breathe. Breathe.

When I'm in control of myself again I continue. "It was chaos. Alarms, smoke, and the sounds of explosions that were too close for comfort. We were trained on doing an evacuation but none of us took it seriously. Maybe if I had..."

I shake my head, biting my lip as the emotions swamp my thoughts again.

"Okay," he says, one of our shared words.

It's oddly comforting and reassuring in a way that single word should never be able to convey but he makes it work.

"No," I say, shaking my head. "If we'd been more serious, maybe it would have been better. I'll never forget that, now. I was helping my patients to the pods. Even as it was happening, none of us thought it was real.

"It had to be a drill, right? Rosalind had ramped up the scenarios, made them more real, so we would take them seriously. The entire concept of the ship, though, was that those of us living on it would forget we were on one. A mental trick to keep us sane. Except in this case it led to greater insanity, didn't it?"

I sit up and look at him, trying to judge how much of what I'm saying he understands. Probably none of it, but I've never talked about this, and now I can't stop. I can't shut it off, I need to say this to someone. No, not someone, to him. I need him to understand what he's getting with me. I have to open up about this in particular, my failure.

There's understanding and acceptance in his eyes, written across his face. It gives me the courage to keep talking.

"Something exploded. My memories are... broken at this point. They don't flow together but are more like disconnected photographs with gaps between them. Still lifes or something. Flash, bright white, blinding and loud. God, it was so loud.

"My ears were ringing so bad I barely heard the screams. Even my own. Then sliding. I was sliding, the floor tilted, you see. I think that's what happened anyway.

"The ship was breaking up. Something catastrophic had happened. We were almost to the escape pods, but almost didn't count. Close didn't save her. The patient I was helping, she was an older woman who could barely move.

"I still see her. She's sliding away, reaching for me. I had her hand in mine. She's begging. I didn't hear her words, but I read her lips, not that I needed to. I know what I'd be saying. Begging, don't let me go. I couldn't."

I choke up and it takes me a moment to get where I can finish the story.

"I lost her, she fell, her mouth open, screaming," tears are streaming down my face, and I choke up again.

He pulls me in with his one arm, pressing my face to his chest. His heart is beating a soothing, double drum rhythm.

"Treasure," he says.

I sob harder, and he repeats the word, over and over until I fall asleep in his arms.

16

URUKOL

I'm lulled by the soft pattering of the rain and the rise and fall of her chest as she sleeps on my chest. I ignore the ache in my broken arm and the itch of my scars. None of that matters now—she has chosen me.

Impossible as it seems, she is mine. My treasure. I will do anything for her, persisting through this discomfort presents no challenge. I would endure an infinity more for her. The fire is burning low and I will need to stoke it soon to keep it from going out, but she is not awake yet. She needs the sleep after the trauma we've been through.

The look on her face when she drove my knife through the skalis' brain warms my heart. Determination, power, she shone with bravery. The fire of a warrior burns in her. My dragon rumbles, satisfied with its choice. She stirs, shifting, and her eyelids flutter.

"Mmm, sorry," she says, sitting up.

My scales are imprinted onto her cheek. It looks like she is partially Zmaj herself. She rubs her face with both hands and shakes herself awake. She says something, words I don't comprehend, then, alert, she looks at me.

"Hungry," she says, patting her stomach.

"Yes, I will cook," I say, but the look on her face makes it clear she doesn't understand.

I motion to the fire then hold my hand up with a finger extended. I want her to know I will cook for her. I don't have my utensils here, but I think I can make her something more than smoked meat, food I hope she will enjoy.

Even the idea of preparing food for her fills me with excitement. I want to please her palate as she gave pleasure to my body. I want to give her everything. The world if she asks for it. She is the most perfect female in the universe, and she chose me. I will spend the rest of my days honoring her for her choice.

She nods which I hope means she understands. I stand up and walk into the jungle. This close to a pool should be a good place for the herbs I've got in mind. After walking around the bole of a tree, I crouch down and move aside the leaves a fern, looking for my prize.

It takes time, but I find them at last without having to go fully out of sight of Leah. I harvest the leaves of the herb carefully and return to her. I stoke up the fire until it's burning well, then I get out the smoked meat. I take it to the water and thrust the meat in, letting it soak up some water. Finishing that, I return to Leah and carefully work the leaves of the herb across it. I knead the pieces of meat, softening it while working the oil from the herb into its texture.

Once I'm satisfied, I find some sticks and rig a structure over the flames and lay the meat out over it to warm. It isn't long before the smoked meat is dripping onto the fire. The spicy scent of the herb mixes with the juice creating an enticing aroma. I smile when I see Leah's eyes widen and her mouth open. She says something that sounds approving.

She reaches for the meat, but I stop her. It needs a little longer to fully come into its own. I shake my head, and she frowns before sitting down. The silence is comfortable, yet I want to talk with her.

She said so much last night before she fell asleep. I couldn't under-stand the words, but I felt her pain.

Pain I want to take away but that is impossible. I could only be there for her, love her, and let her share her burden with me. I must learn her language. This inability to speak to her is not acceptable. How can I care for her and not be able to understand every nuance of every syllable she says?

I close my eyes and inhale deeply, savoring the scents of the meat. It's finished. The aroma signals its perfection. My smile is so wide it hurts my cheeks, but I know she's going to love this. I snatch the meat from the fire and toss it in my hands until it's the right temperature. When I offer it to her, she takes it without hesitation.

My scales tingle in anticipation. She raises the meat to her mouth slowly, deliberately, her delicate, soft lips closing around the strip as her mouth closes. Her jaw tenses as her teeth tear through and her eyes widen in surprise.

"OH!" she exclaims then she shoves the rest of the piece of meat into her mouth.

She groans, closes her eyes, and makes pleasure noises that aren't dissimilar to the ones she made during our lovemaking. She waves her hands towards her mouth, smiling and chewing at the same time.

"Wow!" she exclaims.

My heart leaps as electric chills race across my scales. I nod with great enthusiasm. Happiness is a bubble in my chest swelling until it must burst. She swallows the meat, and I offer her more. She takes one piece and this one she chews slower. It's obvious she's savoring and enjoying it. She says a lot of words but none of them make sense. I smile and nod as if I understand.

She finishes the meat and turns down more when I offer it. Warmth suffuses my limbs. The pleasure of seeing her enjoyment is all the sustenance I need to live on forever. I know I will do anything to experience that again and again.

Now, though, we need to travel. Getting her out of the storm, which is thankfully holding in a lull, and to safety is all that matters. Also when we're home, I can cook for her with proper tools and equipment. I will make feasts for her every day.

A vigor for life fills me. I haven't felt it in so long, it's unrecognizable at first. As it comes clear and I know it for what it is, all the scars of my past, the pain of betrayals, no longer matter. The future is so bright, it has become a sun of its own. Burning away the losses in the promise it offers.

Tomorrows without number, all spent with her. Brighter than any sun, more radiant than the brightest star, my shining beacon. What could I not endure for one hint of her smile?

Nothing. I will get her to safety

Then I will create a home for her from the gifts of Tajss. No matter the betrayal of the Order, the balance of Tajss has been set to rights, and she will give to us who held her faith.

I gather the few possessions that we've managed to keep and point the direction we need to go. We're not far. If the storm will hold off a day, we should make it, barring further incident. She holds her hand out, and I take it.

I can't help but marvel at the feel of it in my hand. Small, delicate, with what I know to be surprising strength. Her hand in mine is a joy and pleasure I never expected in my life. Even the world around us seems brighter. The colors more vivid, the depths are deeper.

My hearts pump faster even as I look around us making sure of my bearings. The leaves glisten with drops of rain, sparking rainbows from the stray rays of sunshine that have escaped the overbearing clouds above. Even the smells of the jungle are vibrant, filling my nostrils with the scents of fresh dirt and life.

A bird sings above, and it's as if the bird is expressing his joy at my own. A beautiful song that complements the music of my soul. She looks up towards the sound with her smile brightening the world.

"Its singing is inspired by you," I say.

Her cheeks blush a rosy pink color. She probably doesn't know exactly what I said, but it's okay. Soon we will have time, and I will learn her language, and if she wants, I will teach her mine. Our future is going to be glorious.

The wind picks up, rustling the trees. Leaves drop down around us as it increases then the rain resumes. Obviously, our luck isn't going to hold as long as I'd hoped. I put my arm around her shoulders and then open my one wing, using it to shield her from the worst of it.

We move faster, slower than I'd like, but her legs aren't as long as mine. Already she's taking two strides for every one of mine. We make our way through the jungle. The good part of the rain coming back is that almost all predators will be sheltering it out.

A lot of the worst predators will hibernate through the worst of the rainy season. It's a terrible time to hunt. Most hunt by smell and the rain makes that almost impossible. She slips as we work our way around the base of a large tree.

She catches herself on the rough bark, and the scent of her blood tangs the air. She yelps, jerking her hand back while I steady her. She holds her hand up for inspection where she's scraped it. Blood wells in the dirty wound, trying to rinse out the grit and filth.

I stop to find a large leaf and form it into a cup in my hand. I hold it up and let the rain fill it, then use the water to rinse her wound. Once the grit is out, I try to wrap the leaf around her hand, but I can't manage it with only one hand of my own. She sees what I am doing and helps, holding the leaf with her other hand, and working together, the makeshift bandage goes into place. I tuck the edges of it under itself to lock it down.

She touches the leaf, staring at it for overly long. When she looks up, there's a softness on her face that makes my cock ache with needs that this is no time or place for. Her lips curl up as if they're moving in slow motion. A light burns in her eyes, and there is no need for words between us.

Words can't convey the feelings, they couldn't possibly contain the depths and heights of the sensations she creates. My dragon rumbles with satisfaction. She is the one, and she is mine as much as I am hers. Hers to command, forever.

"We should move," I say, the words emerge with reluctance.

I have no desire to move. I don't want to break this moment. I want it to last forever. She nods, either from understanding or empathy. Reluctantly, I lead the way. The jungle is thick with undergrowth that we have to fight our way through, making it slow going.

She displays her strength as we work together to make progress. Some areas she's able to slip through without problem, where I must bully my way past. As we move there are so many special moments. Moments where she touches my arm, she smiles, or her face glows with a delight that sets my heart and balls on fire.

Dreams of our future play out through my thoughts while we travel. It makes the time pass fast. I'm so caught up in my own pleasure of being with her that I almost miss the danger until it is too late. She catches it before I do.

I'm holding a branch up for her to move under, when she stops and turns back the way we've come. The tension makes her vibrate with an energy of anticipation and fear. It's obvious she heard something, so instead of asking I listen.

A branch snaps, and then I hear voices. Voices, did the others come looking for us? I open my mouth to call out, but she puts a hand on my chest. Her eyes are wide, her mouth turned down in a frown, and she's trembling.

I snap my mouth shut. Fear. I strain to hear the voices, and my own hearts race in response. Those aren't the voices of the ones we were separated from.

"I'm sick to death of these patrols," a voice says, drifting across the soaked jungle.

"Quit complaining, you know what the Eye would say," another voice says.

They sound familiar, but I can't place names with them. One thing I'm sure of though, they are from the Order. The Order that evicted me in my wounded state and left me for dead. She's terrified of them too.

I have every reason in the world not to trust the Order, and it seems she does as well. I take hold of her arm and move her past the branch, then slowly lower it so that it doesn't make any excessive noise.

She presses herself against me, staring in the direction of the voices. She's shaking with fear. The dragon rises and red covers my thoughts and vision as the bijass reacts. I ball my hands into fists so tight my claws draw blood. My tail rises between my shoulders, and I'm ready to attack.

No.

Don't be stupid. They outnumber me. No matter my fury, I can't be assured I'll win. There are at least two of them. One of them could steal her while the other kept me busy. Fighting is not the answer, no matter how much the dragon wants to destroy them for making her feel fear.

I touch her shoulder and she looks up. I put my hand over my mouth, and she nods. Then I point to the path we've been following. She indicates her understanding, and we carefully pick our way through the trees.

I use my tail to stir the leaves behind us, covering over our trail the best I can. The voices are growing louder, they're coming closer. We need a place to hide, now. I stop and peer into the dimly lit jungle, looking for anything that will serve, and spot a fallen tree.

Moss and various plants grow along the length of it. It's going to be our best hope of a place to hide. I point to our goal and then let her lead the way to it so I can continue obscuring our trail. A good tracker will not be fooled, but in this case, I can do no more. If I must fight, I will, but better to play smart.

We reach the far side of the log. There's a small gap beneath it, she lies down flat on her own and slides into the space. I lie down outside it, too large to fit with her, and wait. The voices grow louder.

My hearts beat loud in my ears and blood rushes to my head. The red covering my vision darkens, growing thicker, and it's becoming harder to think clearly. Single thoughts pound with the pulsing of my hearts.

Kill. Destroy. Protect.

Over and over. My breathing becomes shallow, and it's harder to hold myself still. The desire to leap into action, surprise my enemies and destroy them consumes me. I struggle with the primal instincts of the bijass as the enemy moves closer.

I look to the side and my eyes lock with hers. The bijass recedes slightly. She's scared but controlled. She's not letting fear rule her, how can I do any less? She sets the example, easing my own struggle.

"There's nothing here, this is stupid," one of the voices says.

"Shut up, you're stupid," the other responds.

"Nice," the first voice says. "Mighty come back there."

"You want to be sent to Zirthoan and JKaran when we return?" the other voice asks.

"No," the first voice says, and I hear his fear.

Zirthoan and Jkaran. The dragon rages, rattling the chains I've barely managed to use to hold it down. They're the ones who left me, wounded and dying. They laughed. I hear their laughter echoing in my ears still from when they left me to die.

They're coming closer. Leah's face pales, her eyes widen, and she covers her mouth with her hand. I slide my hand across the dirt and take her free one in mine. It sounds like one of them is directly on the opposite side of the fallen tree. It's large enough that I should be hidden but I can't be sure. My muscles tense, ready to react in an instant. I hold my breath waiting.

"Anything over there?"

"No," the fearful one answers.

He kicks something and it slams against the fallen tree with a crack that echoes through the wet jungle.

"What about on the other side of that tree? You look for tracks over there?"

"Do I look stupid?" he asks.

Be stupid. Be stupid.

"We need to meet the rest of the group back at the rendezvous, let's go."

"Right," the closer one says.

There's a scratching and scrabbling sound. I look up, hearts pounding in my throat, and see his outline appear past the edge of the tree. He's looking out across the jungle. If he looks down, I won't be able to hide.

Leah squeezes my hand, but I don't dare move even my eyes. I can't tear them away from watching him, so close. If he looks down, I'll leap up. If I can hit him fast enough, I might be able to catch the other one before he can escape.

Then what? There are even more members of the Order out here searching. They must be searching for Leah and the other aliens. They're certainly not looking for me, they all think I'm dead. In all this time we haven't seen any signs of the Order. They've left us outcasts to our own devices and never come this close to our home.

This is bad on so many levels. We are not strong enough to take on the Order. If they are hunting the females, then it's not only a concern for Leah, but for my brothers, and for the rest of her kind as well.

The Zmaj on the log shakes his head, his wings rustle, and he turns and disappears from sight. He pauses, his back towards us, and starts to turn back around.

"Come on!" the other voice yells.

He disappears from sight, and I release my held breath. I don't move yet. Leah and I wait, straining our senses to make sure they are gone. I don't know how long we lie there, waiting to be certain. Rainwater is pooling beneath me when at last I rise and peek over the fallen tree.

Nothing.

I stand and look in all directions until I'm sure we're alone, for now. Kneeling, I hold my hand out and help Leah emerge from her hiding place. She radiates nervous energy as her head swivels around, making sure for herself.

She puts her hands on my chest, palms flat and warm against my scales. I cover her hands with mine and tilt my head down until my forehead rests against hers. It's a stolen moment, and all that we have. The urgency to get to the others is exponentially greater.

She looks up, kisses me, and we move. Hand in hand, we travel as quick as possible. The wind is cold, and the rain is coming harder yet again. The lull of the storm is ending. There's no stopping for shelter though. We're being hunted. The jungle was dangerous enough before I knew that the Order was this close to us, now the dangers of the jungle itself no longer compare. Our best hope is to avoid capture and reach the others.

We've been climbing steadily for a long time, which is good. The area is becoming familiar looking, even if there are no landmarks that stand out yet. I know I'm heading in the right direction for home. It's obvious we've gone further away than I had thought originally though.

"STOP!"

The command is authoritative and loud, echoing off the trees but leaving no doubt of its intended target. My body stops without thought, even now the training of the Order is ingrained in me. Obey orders. Do not hesitate, do not think, do as commanded.

Leah has no such conditioning, she runs. The proper response of course. She jerks me into motion, breaking the command of years of training. A glance over my shoulder and I spot four Zmaj racing through the jungle, chasing us.

I sweep Leah into my one good arm and run.

17

LEAH

I've pains in parts of my body I didn't know could hurt. I'm out of breath and my heart is pounding but I can't stop now. Shit, it's the Order. Does Urukol know what they want me for? I don't know if Angota had a chance to tell him.

"Yipp!" I exclaim as I'm swept off my feet.

Urukol scoops me up in his good arm without missing a step. I turn in and wrap my arms around his neck and my legs around his waist. Trees blur around us as he runs flat out. Jumping over fallen limbs, dodging low branches, barreling through brush.

Our pursuers shout as they chase, calling out. I hear multiple voices, at least six, maybe more. We're moving so fast it's making me nauseated. I close my eyes and grit my teeth, trying to keep my stomach under control.

The wind blows harder, and I shiver as rain pelts against me. Urukol's speed is incredible. He's so strong and nimble, bounding through the jungle with ease. He's amazing, but it's not going to be good enough. The Zmaj chasing are closing on us.

It can't end like this. We only found each other, the end of our story can't be this. I know he won't let them take me, not if he's alive. If they do capture me… I'm not going to be a breeder. I'll do anything, but not that.

An hour ago I was daydreaming about having babies with Urukol. Ziva confided in me that she thinks Riley is pregnant, and obviously the Zmaj think our races are compatible. Why else would they want us as 'breeders'?

No. I'm not going to end that way. Either we survive together or neither of us make it. I'm not going to live in this world without him. He's the best thing that's ever happened to me, and I'm not going to let it go.

My resolve calms the churning of my stomach. This ends one of two ways and knowing that, being fully resigned to it, brings an unexpected calm. I kiss Urukol's cheek. He won't know why, but it doesn't matter. I want him to feel my love, to have some small gesture to know how much I love and appreciate him.

Suddenly he's sliding to a stop, his feet backpedaling so fast they're a blur. In surprise, I look ahead. My stomach lurches and I almost lose its contents. We're on the edge of a cliff, one he barely kept from running off the edge of.

It drops at least a hundred feet. Far enough that I can't see the bottom in the pouring rain. Urukol spins around, and my stomach drops down seeing the Zmaj of the Order closing on our position. They've got us surrounded leaving no way to escape. Urukol says something that sounds like a curse. He turns to the cliff and looks down.

"No, no, no, no," I say over and over shaking my head.

He can't be thinking it, we can't jump, we'll never survive it. He looks over his shoulder at the Zmaj warriors closing on us. Each of them carries one of their unique weapons, lochabers, with wicked sharp blades that seem to glint in the nonexistent sun.

Watching them approach, time slows. They jump and leap forward, gliding through the air. The encroaching line almost moves in a kind of unison, a musical arrangement of impending doom closing on us. My heart races. I'm panting with trepidation.

Urukol looks at the cliff where it drops away below his feet. One last glance over his shoulder, and I see the determination on his face. My scream hasn't left my lips before he's moving. I watch in dawning horror as his foot steps off the edge and hangs over the nothingness.

My stomach lurches, then falls faster than the two of us. He twists in the air and all I can do is tighten my grip and pray. Wind rushes past my ears, carrying away my scream. We drop at least ten feet when he loosens his grip on me and reaches for the rocks speeding past. He grabs one, and we jerk to a stop.

"Ugh," he grunts in pain.

I stop screaming for the first time since this insane adventure. The only sounds are the wind whistling past and the claws of his feet scrabbling to find purchase. His chest is heaving as we hang, twisting from side to side as the wind buffets against us.

Shouts above us, and I look up. The Zmaj are looking over the edge and arguing with each other. None of them seem willing to follow us, at least not readily. The problem now is what do we do? I have no idea what Urukol's plan is but no matter what it is, it's insane. How long can he hold on like this?

He looks up, then down, and then from side to side. As he looks past me our eyes lock for a moment. He grins. It's a total 'I've got this,' look on his face. Incredibly, I feel better. My doubts and fears fade in the light of that look. The butterflies storming the ramparts of my stomach ease, and the bile drops out of my throat. I put my faith in the only place I can, him.

He moves his hand down to a different crevasse and then lowers us down as his foot finds a new purchase. One hand, one foot at a time, he works us down the cliff towards a bottom that we can't see. A thick fog churns below, obscuring the ground.

Small rocks rain down, hitting me in the head. I glance up and two of the Zmaj are climbing over the edge. They're moving slow but obviously aren't going to give up. I close my eyes and focus on breathing.

One movement at a time, Urukol keeps working us down. The fact he's doing it one handed and carrying my weight on top of that is incredible. Obviously a Zmaj looks strong, they're all buff and muscular, but most human men who are big like this wouldn't have this kind of stamina to back it up. It's incredible.

He's got this. He's got me. Trust him.

It's perhaps the hardest thing I've ever had to do in my life. I'm not only putting my trust in him, or my metaphorical heart, I'm putting my actual life in his one good arm. It has to work because what other choice is there? Let go and jump? Not happening. I've got too much to live for, I can't even tell him how I feel yet!

SCREECH!

The screech is deafening. My ears ring, and my heartbeat is pounding in my throat, making the blood in my ears every bit as loud. Terror creates cold chills as my muscles lock, and I can barely force my head to turn to look.

One of those monstrously huge lizard-bird crossbred creatures that Angota fought at our first home dives towards the cliff.

My stomach clenches and I bite my tongue. The thing opens its mouth and another loud screech pierces my head as it opens its massive wings. The span of them looks at big as two Zmaj standing on each other's shoulders. The wings slow its descent, its clawed feet extend as it barrels towards us.

Urukol looks at it, up at our pursuers, then to the other side. He lets go of the wall and leaps. We're flying through the air, but I can't watch. I keep my eyes clenched shut until we jerk to a stop at the same time someone scrapes across the rock wall of the cliff.

I know I'm screaming, but I can't hear it over the ringing and pounding of my pulse. I force my eyes open when we stop falling. We're hanging by a vine, drifting slightly back and forth, slowly twisting one way then the other.

The bird-thing is climbing back into the air, but I'm sure it hasn't given up on its meal so easily. Shouts echo down to us lest I forget that we're also being pursued by the Order. This gets better and better.

Suddenly we drop a few feet and I scream. We come to a jerking halt as he gets his grip on the vine again. He swings his tail, bringing us closer to the rock wall, and he reaches out with his legs, trying to find purchase with his feet.

His claws scratch on the stone, but we drift away again before he can find a hold. The two members of the Order are making faster time down than we are in getting away. They're closing in faster than should be possible, except they have two arms each and aren't carrying a me.

Urukol is watching them, then turns his head at some sound behind us. I look in the direction he is, and the bird-thing drops out of a cloud aiming at one of the Order. The Zmaj doesn't see it in time or can't do anything if he does. The monster's claws snatch him from the wall and it takes off. The Zmaj's screams fade into the distance.

I squeeze my eyes shut tight and try to block out the sound. Bile rises in my throat. We could be next.

Urukol doesn't give any signs of letting it bother him. He's swinging his tail making our swing wider until the cliff wall is coming towards us again. He sticks his feet out, and then the claws of his toes are scraping against the rock, scrabbling for any crevasse.

He doesn't find one, and we're swinging out from the wall again. He looks up and I do too. Another of the Zmaj are coming over the edge, and the one that remains from before is making fast progress towards us.

Urukol growls and it rumbles in his chest vibrating against me. He looks at me and something in his eyes frightens me. Resolve and a daring, he can't be thinking...

We drop.

Fast.

I'm screaming but the wind steals the sound long before I hear it. The fog below races closer and closer. I cling to him with every ounce of strength I can muster. In seconds we pass into the fog and the world is nothing but gray-white nothingness.

Am I dead?

I might be, maybe this is what it is. Nothingness and screams. My lungs burn, my muscles tremble. Surely, I'm not dead. I wouldn't be clinging to him still in death, would I?

In response, I'm jerked so hard my grip on him slips, and I slide off his neck.

"LEAH!" he screams, his voice cracking.

Desperately trying to grip him, I catch around his waist. Eyes clenched tight, I clench my jaw and force myself to breathe. I'm alive. We're alive. Thank all that might ever have been holy in the universe, we're alive. Barely daring, I crack one eye open and look at him.

"Don't. Ever. Do. That. Again."

He may not understand my words, but the meaning gets through to him. He grins and shakes his head very slightly. His tail hooks under my ass giving me support to help claw my way back up to his neck.

I can't see our pursuers any longer, nor can I see what lies below us. We're hanging in a gray nothingness. My heart slows and my breathing comes to something resembling normal. Once I'm wrapped around him with arms and legs, he swings his tail and resumes trying to get to the wall.

Four attempts later, we're perched against it and he works us down. It's impossible to measure time or distance. The fog grows thicker the lower we go, until even the sounds of the world are muted and distant.

All the world that was is fading as we pass into this nether realm. A world that consists of only the two of us and no others. It's crazy knowing that we're literally hanging by his one hand, but I'm calm. Almost... serene.

He's got this. He's got me. I'm safe because I'm with him, and no matter what the world throws at us, we'll face and overcome it together.

He continues working us down the cliff face. One motion at a time as he grunts with effort, but never once does he falter. There's no hint of the exhaustion he has to be feeling. I rest my face against the rough scars where the top of his wing should be and do my best to not make this harder than it is.

There's no sign of an end. Maybe this cliff goes on forever. It feels like it does, but then what else is there? With no points of orientation, nothing to measure anything against, the only choice is to keep going.

A Zmaj voice yells something from above us. Urukol pauses, clinging to the cliff and catching his breath. The voice yells again, more words. The only thing I catch is 'female' out of it, but that's enough for me to guess the rest of the sentence.

They're telling him they only want me. They'll let him go if he turns me over. He shakes his head, but I don't need even that sign. He'll never give me up. I'm his and he's mine. He grunts and resumes the climb down.

"AHHHH!" a scream muffled by the thick fog comes from above, and then rocks pelt us.

I duck my head and Urukol does the same, as the pebbles and dirt bounce off us. The scream continues, coming closer. I open my eyes as a large form falls past, arms, legs and tail grasping at the empty air.

One of the Zmaj fell, which is a sobering fact. That man, with two good arms and no extra human clinging to him, fell.

We got this. We got this. I'm fine. He's fine.

Urukol grunts as the other warrior screams his way past and unperturbed continues our descent. The fog thins until at last I see ground. We're so close! Maybe thirty or forty feet more to go. He glances down and nods as if to himself.

SCREECH!

"Oh shit," I curse.

That bird-thing is back for seconds. I look in all directions trying to spot it first. Please go after the other guys, please go after them.

Urukol doesn't wait though. He kicks off of the cliff face and we're swinging through the air freely. I tighten my grip on his neck as we arc out and around. We come to a stop on a small ledge. He presses me against it right as the creature dives out of the clouds over our head. Its clawed feet are extended, ready to snatch him away.

I drop to the cliff, pressing myself against the face as much as possible. He pulls the knife from his waist and shifts around to face the creature. He slashes at the thing as it extends those wicked claws. The knife makes a small slice and the monster pulls its claws back, beating its wings as it reverses directions, pulling up.

Urukol widens his stance and shifts so that he's covering me with his body. He scans the sky above, knife held ready.

The screech comes again, and I cover my ears but force my eyes to stay open. I want to see what's happening. The thing dives, beak first, then whips its wings open at the last instant, trying to snatch him.

He twists so that the claws go on either side and stabs at the body. He misses, but the thing stabs with its beak. The two of them are fighting while the bird creature hovers. Beak, claw, claw, beak broken by Urukol stabbing and slashing. He blocks a claw from reaching me by thrusting his arm between it and me.

The claw closes on his arm and the bird flies backwards. He's jerked forward, off balance. He swings with the makeshift cast on his other arm, slamming it against the thing's leg.

The creature screams in pain or frustration, then jerks forward again. Urukol is dragged to the edge. I grab his waist and pull back. My feet skid across loose gravel—we're both going to the edge.

Urukol acts without hesitation. He slides his tail between us and pushes me back to the cliff wall, then leaps forward before I can get a fresh hold.

He's swinging from the thing's grip as it fights to gain altitude, carrying him away from me.

"NO!" I scream, reaching towards him, desperate to pull him back.

The creature pulls him up, and they disappear into the fog. I'm alone. Stuck on a cliff face stunned. Staring up at the light gray fog where the love of my life disappeared.

18

URUKOL

*M*y arm is going numb in the anzilu's grip. It's all I can do to keep my grip on the knife. I can't lose that, it's my only chance to survive this. I must return to Leah.

When I pull myself up, my broken arm throbs with pain, but I don't have a choice. Curling my arm until I lift myself up level with the things claw, I grab its leg with my broken arm. Pain shoots through the arm. Stars form in my vision but the bijass rises in response. Red haze drowns the pain.

Leah is in danger. She needs me. Protect.

Pushing past the pain, I twist myself around until I shift the knife to my bad arm. Good arm free, I twist around until I have a solid grip on the anzilu's leg. Any moment now it's going to drop me. That's the normal way that they feed. Carry their prey up to a good height, drop it onto the rocks below and then feed on the carcass.

I'm ready when it does. I don't fall and it screeches in anger and surprise. It bends its long neck, snapping at me.

I curl my tail around its neck, wrapping it around and choking it. Its long beak opens wide, revealing row after row of sharp yellowed teeth. It screeches in my face, deafening me, but that's the last of its air.

It struggles to inhale while also trying to stay in the air. I'm not done with it. I let go with my hand. I'm dangling upside down by my tail around its neck.

I swing back and forth, easing the grip of my tail when I get enough swing going, and I go up and around. When I reach the apex of my swing, I let my tail hold go and drop onto its back. It cries out, bucking.

I lean forward and grab its neck with my good arm and pull back. It bucks, fighting, and trying to knock me off.

I hold tight, letting it fight. I want it to wear itself out, use its own energy against it. My only goal now is to ride it out.

We soar through the air, rising up while it bucks and fights. It goes into a roll, over and over, but I use my tail to keep myself on its back, even while we're upside down. My single wing catches at the wind rushing past, creating drag that should help wear it down.

It closes its wings and goes into a dive. Wind rips against me, pulling and causing me to lift from its back. Pulling my tail tighter, I jerk myself flat against it. Briefly I see Leah on the cliff as the creature dives to the ground.

She is radiantly beautiful, and the sight of her infuses strength into my muscles. The dragon roars seeing its claim, and I can't contain its joy. I let it out in a long, joyous bellow. I'm more alive than I've been in lifetimes.

The ground rushes closer and closer. We'll hit soon if it doesn't pull up, but I trust in its survival instincts. Sure enough, right before impact, it opens its wings, and we glide over the ground which is so close I could reach out and touch it if I wanted.

We climb back into the air, but the fight is going out of it. The climb is slow, steady but it's no longer bucking and fighting against my taking control. By the time we pass Leah again, it's hardly fighting me at all.

I pull its head to the left and it shifts to glide that direction. I experiment, pulling one way then the other, and it responds to my commands. I pull up and we rise, push down and it dives. The fight is gone, I've broken its spirit.

No Zmaj has ever done such a thing. I shift around, dangling my legs around its long neck and letting the death grip of my tail and one arm go. I wait for it to react to my loosened control. Prepared to move if it fights or tries to buck me off, but nothing. It's docile, or close enough.

I lift my fist in the air and roar in triumph.

Pushing down on its head, I guide it towards Leah, ready to rescue my love. When we emerge from the cloud bank, she sees, and her eyes widen while a smile spreads across her gorgeous face. She cheers, throwing her arms in the air and jumping up and down on the treacherous cliff.

I guide the anzilu next to her using my knees.

"JUMP!" I yell, holding out my hand as we drop past her.

She doesn't hesitate, throwing herself off the cliff in an act of utter faith. I catch her with my good arm and swing her around behind. She settles herself, and we glide the rest of the way to the ground. The anzilu accepts my control and direction without fighting.

As the ground zooms closer, Leah tightens her grip and buries her face against my wing. The anzilu pulls back, extending its legs to land. Leah yelps as we're leaned back then it touches down, running until it loses momentum.

It screeches, extending its neck and flapping its wings. Leah has a death grip around my middle, so I let go of the anzilu and slide down its back until I'm on my own two feet. She lowers herself off my back, but I keep myself between her and the creature.

I'm not sure what it's going to do now that I'm not directly controlling it. It walks forward, an odd waddle that lacks any grace, wings wide as it turns around to me. I stand ready to fight if I must. It caws, not a full-on screech, raising its long beak high and snapping at the air.

Out of the corner of my eye I see the fallen warriors' remains. I keep Leah behind me as I move toward the remains. The anzilu's beady eyes track my movement. Once I'm beside the remains I point at it then down at the remains.

It caws and waddles over. I move us away, and then the anzilu feasts on the remains. It's a noisy, nasty affair that Leah does not need to see. I turn my back on it and block her view with my body.

"Urukol," she says my name, resting her head against my chest.

I wrap my arm around her and hold her tight, ignoring the sounds of the beast's meal. We're safe, for now. The Zmaj from the Order aren't likely to try and reach us any longer. They've already lost too much to justify the attempt.

We need to get to my home. The others needs to know that the Order is close, and I want to know they're safe as well. I cup Leah's face and she looks up.

"Go," I say, nodding my head behind us.

She nods understanding. The sounds of the anzilu's feasting finish and it caws, but doesn't fly away. I turn to face it and find it staring at me as if it's waiting. There's a cold intelligence to those eyes I never would have suspected.

"Go," I point up and away.

It follows my pointing finger then looks back to me. It caws loudly, flapping its wings and puffing its chest out. I point again and order it to go. It caws and bobs its head three times, then backs up. It flaps its wings faster and faster until it lifts off the ground. It caws loudly, and I would swear it looks back as it flies away.

Strange.

I have no more time to give to such possibilities. It's raining harder again, and the wind is increasing its force. Soon the fury of the storm will return, again. I stare up the cliff trying to make sure of my assumption that the Order will not risk it, but a thick cloud hides them if they are trying.

Leah shivers violently. The wind is colder, and it makes my muscles sluggish and they ache. Finding shelter and waiting it out would be best but it's not the smart move. We can't be here where the Order knows we came down or anywhere near it. They may not try the cliff again, but they will work their way around.

If the Eye wants the females, they aren't going to give up. Returning to the Eye, empty-handed, when they had one of them in their sights will not go well for them. A fact I know too well. The Order is corrupt at its core. The ideals I joined it to support are given only lip service by those who lead.

I hold out my hand, and Leah takes it. As my hand closes on hers it hits me fully for the first time. My disfigurement hasn't stopped me from protecting her.

I've cared for my treasure, protected her, kept her safe in the most extraordinary of circumstances. I have tamed an anzilu, the most dangerous predator of this continent. We've escaped the Order. Every threat imaginable has come our way and she is safe.

I am a male.

A sensation burns through my body like fire racing through my veins. Pride swells, my one wing opens wide and my tail rises between my shoulders. Leah looks at me and her face is beaming, alight with love.

My love for her is boundless. The dragon roars and I can't contain it. I throw my head back and let out my triumphant roar, giving the dragon its voice. I throw my arms wide, the pain of the broken one barely noticeable.

Leah places her hands on my chest and I scoop her up with my good arm. Her lips, soft and succulent, press to mine. My cock pounds, ready to explode at her touch. She wraps her legs around my waist and then she leans her head back too and we roar together.

She laughs and I am laughing with her. The rain pours down, soaking us through, but nothing matters because we are together. We are one.

19

LEAH

*M*y head is throbbing. All I can do is focus on this moment and keep pushing forward. I can't believe what I've been through, what we've done. My muscles quiver with exhaustion, but they keep working.

I'm sure that Urukol can't feel any better than I do. He carried me down that cliff with one arm. It's unbelievable, I don't know if the other girls will believe me when I tell them. Unreal. Incredible.

It's love.

Warmth deep in my belly pulses, and I'm drawing all my strength from it. What else do I call this? I'm a nurse, it's not a physical thing, no organ or body part that feels like this or creates these sensations. It's much, much more, the human spirit maybe. Or, more accurately, love.

I love him, and I know he loves me too.

So we keep moving. Climbing over loose rocks as the ground inclines back up. Rivulets of water speed pass, joining together and becoming a stream. The rain keeps coming harder. Every time I think it's reached a peak, it figures out a way to rain harder. The wind isn't as bad as it has been, but I know that can change in an instant.

Head down, hair plastered to my face, clothes sticking, it's one foot then another. One step, the next, and the next. I'm too tired to look up, and only glance behind us when the itching on the back of my neck becomes too intense to ignore.

Urukol has his arm around my waist giving me support, and I hate it, but I'm leaning against his strength. We travel until the gray world becomes dark, and still we continue. I'm so tired I can hardly stay upright.

The rain beats against us, the wind is howling louder. We've made our way back into the jungle, and we're no longer climbing at least. Urukol stops, raising a hand to shield his eyes. I do the same, but his eyesight is far superior. All I see is dark jungle which doesn't allow me to see very far at all.

"LEAH!" Ziva's voice emerges from the blackness.

It can't be! My breath catches in my throat as my heart leaps into double time. I stumble forward. I've lost it. It's my imagination.

"Oh Leah!" Ziva calls again, and a shadowy figure carrying a torch runs around a tree.

"Ziva?" I ask.

The continuously pouring rain hides my tears of relief and joy. Ziva throws her arms around me, and a moment later all the other survivors surround us. Angota and Rakstan join them, and the group helps us forward.

They lead us to a path that ascends between two large trees. Passing to the other side, it angles up a cliff face, turning back and forth, until we reach a wide flat cliff. A heavy leather hangs against the wall. We pass through the leather, and for the first time since I can remember, the rain stops.

Urukol stays by my side, but the passage we're in isn't wide enough for both of us. He steps ahead and leads the way. Everyone is talking at once. It's a cacophony of words and noise. I hear it all, but it's a white noise, I can't make sense of it.

Someone wraps a blanket around my shoulders and guides me to a seat. I huddle over on myself, shivering so hard my teeth are chattering. They position Urukol on a seat in front of me, wrapping warm leathers around him as well.

Our eyes lock, and despite the chattering, I smile. As one we reach towards each other, and his big hand closes on mine.

"Ah seriously?" Michael asks.

I hear someone punch him, and he grunts. "Shut up," Mick hisses.

Everyone is looming around us. Shuffling around each other, pushing and pulling, but it's all peripheral. Urukol leans closer until our foreheads are touching. I close my eyes and wait for the warmth to penetrate my bones.

Someone stokes up a fire, casting orange light and causing shadows to dance around us. Urukol wraps his arm around my shoulders. I welcome its weight, it's comforting.

"Treasure," he whispers.

My heart races at the single word that I do understand. A single word that carries with it a breadth of meaning and intention that no language barrier can hinder. Warmth flushes across my body as I wrap my arms around his neck and kiss him.

"Can you help with this please?" Asia asks.

"Sure," I say, putting down the thin strips of wood I'm attempting to weave into a basket.

"Put your finger there," Asia instructs, and I do as she asks.

She ties off the leather strip that finishes a new container.

"Thanks," she says and gives me a smile.

Clickity, clickity, clickity, clickity.

The sound of the knife is rhythmic, almost musical. I look over my shoulder and watch Urukol chopping the vegetables. Even with his broken arm, the speed and accuracy of his prep is so fast it is incredible.

He scoops the orange and green vegetable into the pan he has heating over the stove. A scent similar to lemon tinged with ginger fills the air. My mouth is watering in an instant. Asia looks up and now her smile is radiant.

"Oh wow," she says.

"Right?" I ask.

Urukol looks at us and holds up a finger, indicating we should wait. He tosses the pan making the vegetables sizzle loudly. He picks up a thick strip of meat and lays it down in the pan. It crackles as it touches, then the smells filling the room become a cornucopia of delight. There are layers to the smells that I can't interpret in any way except my stomach's grumbling with a hunger I didn't realize I felt, and my mouth's watering.

"You've got a keeper," Asia says.

"I'll admit it, I'm jealous," Mick says coming out of the rear storage area. "That smells amazing."

I smile, but I can barely take my eyes off Urukol. His scars are sexy. The way he deftly handles the knife, and he can cook? What isn't there to be in love with? Butterflies dance in my stomach just looking at him.

It's hard to focus, but I force myself to pay attention to the basket I'm weaving.

"How long do you think we have?" Mick asks.

"Couple days?" Asia offers.

"That soon?" Mick asks.

"You want to stay here when we know the Order is close?" I ask.

"I don't want to travel in the rain," Mick says. "You know that better than all of us."

I smile and nod. I don't want to either, but I know, more than any of them probably, that the Zmaj will keep us safe. Urukol will protect me and them.

There's a commotion outside as some of the others return. The three new Zmaj enter first, led by Thargar. Mick's eyes follow him and her lips part as she exhales heavily. I don't miss that look or the smile that forms with it.

The three Zmaj laugh and it's clear, even though I can't speak their language well, that they're giving Urukol a hard time. He smiles and makes a dismissive gesture, waving them away. Angota and Rakstan come in making the small space overly crowded. We can all fit in here, but barely. This home isn't designed for this many people. It was a natural cave that the four Zmaj have turned into a home, but now that they've taken us refugees in, we'll need more space.

Angota talks rapidly and the other Zmaj respond. Ziva and Riley come to the main area from the back, the only two of us who are somewhat fluent in Zmaj, so they're the only ones who can follow the conversation.

"Well?" Mick asks, impatient as ever.

"They've found a place," Riley says. "But it's a long ways off."

"I'm all for a long ways from the Order," Asia says.

"They want to go in small groups," Ziva says.

Cold races down my arms, and my stomach ties into a knot. My mouth is too dry, and my throat too tight to ask my immediate concern.

"Why?" Asia asks.

"The Zmaj want to prepare the place before we arrive and make sure there is a safe trail for us to get there before they hide our tracks," Riley says.

Ziva is frowning with her arms across her chest. She's not happy, and I'm not either. I don't want Urukol to be away for an unknown amount of time. I haven't had the nightmare since we've been together. Maybe it's because I've finally come to terms with it, but I think he's most of it. Even in my sleep, he protects me.

"It's smart," Mick says.

"I don't like it," Ziva says. "We should all go."

"I agree," I say.

Riley talks to the Zmaj and they all speak at once. I may not be able to understand their words, but their tone makes it clear what their thoughts of that position is. It's one big fat no. I look at Ziva and she drops her arms shaking her head. She says something in Zmaj, slowly. She's not fluent like Riley is, but she can get her point across.

Rakstan moves to her and takes her in his arms. Urukol says something, and then the others voice opinions. I'm lost watching them go back and forth, but there's an empty feeling in my guts like I'm on the verge of losing something. Tears form, but I hold them back, I'm not going to give in to an undefined grief. That's ridiculous.

"Only Thargar and Othim are going to go," Riley says. "They'll make sure it's safe first. Then the Zmaj will take turns hauling supplies and doing some construction to make it more comfortable. The rest will remain here to protect us."

I shake with relief and exhale heavily. I'm so thankful, I can't express it in words. While the debate was going on, Urukol has laid out an amazing meal, and we all get our plates to move through the line.

There's light conversation during dinner. Riley and Ziva make sure the Zmaj and all of us are understanding each other. As we wrap up the meal, Riley teaches us all three new words in Zmaj. It's become a custom. Once that is finished, Bahir stands up, clears his throat, then a low rumble emerges.

He has a rich, deep bass voice that fills the room. As he establishes the tune Othim rises and joins him with his full baritone. The two Zmaj weave their voices in and around each other making beautiful music.

I close my eyes and lean against Urukol, listening to the song. The words don't matter, and it seems to my uneducated ear that there barely are any. It's the melody, the soaring notes, that carries me away. It's a song of the future, at least in my head, of possibilities and of hope.

Hope.

A word I didn't know I'd given up on. I was stuck in a state of fear and failure. I knew, analytically, it wasn't my fault what happened, but I couldn't get past it. I still regret it, but sometimes things happen that we can't control.

In the end, though, things work. Fate? Destiny?

What else do I consider it? Lying here, Urukol's arm around me, my cheek resting on his cool scales, if it's not the hand of a higher power, then I don't know what is. I can't fathom random chance would bring me to this exact moment, to the arms of the man who stole my heart.

No. There's much more at work here.

In my mind, I'm soaring into a future. Something resonates inside of me, and I know that I'm home. I've never felt this way before. I'd always thought the ship was home, but that was because I didn't know any better.

No, Tajss is my home. This is where I'm meant to be. Where we are meant to be. This planet, this place is our home. Urukol is my destiny. The future may not be easy, but we'll face it together, and there is no doubt in my mind we will prevail.

There's a commotion, so I open my eyes to see what is happening. Riley races out of the room to the bathroom area, and we all hear her getting sick. Ziva catches my eye. This isn't new and none of us are talking about it, but we all know.

That swell of her belly isn't something that's gone unnoticed. She's pregnant. Which means that we humans can have Zmaj babies. I tilt my head up and Urukol is looking down with a broad smile on his face.

He shifts his hand to my belly. I cover his hand with mine, and imagine what it will be like to have a life growing in my womb. Warmth suffuses my limbs, and I stretch my neck up until he meets me with a kiss.

Maybe tonight will be it. I want a baby too. I want to create the future, for us, and for Tajss.

Want to be the first to know when **the next sexy Zmaj** is ready for you? SUBSCRIBE TO MIRANDA MARTIN'S MAILING LIST

Are you interested in getting the latest updates from Miranda Martin? You'll be automatically welcomed with the subscriber exclusive *Alien Prince*. Once or twice a month, Miranda sends out sneak peeks of works in progress, shiny new covers, hot deals and sales, giveaways and more!

www.mirandarmartinromance.com/newsletter

ABOUT THE AUTHOR

USA Today Bestselling Author of fantasy and scifi romance, Miranda Martin's books feature larger than life heroes with out-of-this-world anatomy and smart heroines destined to save the world. As a little girl she would sneak off with her nose in a book, dreaming of magical realms. Today she brings those fantasies to life and adores every fan who chooses to live in them for a while.

She was born and raised in southern Virginia, but as a veteran she's traveled to places like Korea, Hawaii and good 'ole Texas. Now she's settled in Kansas, the heart of America, with her husband and daughters. Her favorite animals are dragons, unicorns and cats. If she's not writing, you can still find her tucked away somewhere with a warm blanket and her nose in a book.

Get in touch!
mirandamartinromance.com
miranda@mirandamartinromance.com

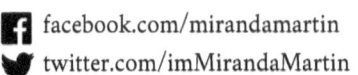

facebook.com/mirandamartin
twitter.com/imMirandaMartin
instagram.com/imMirandaMartin